## "How about if I scream?"

Polly's threat was wild, her body stiffly refusing to yield to the hard lines of his as she fought the leap of her pulses.

Raschid laughed huskily. "They will either think that you are very passionate in my arms or that I am beating you. Neither eventuality will bring them rushing through the doors."

As he captured her mouth again, skilled and unhurried, her body heated to the abrasively masculine line of his. She could not deny him. His breath rasped in his throat as he released her, sinking back to observe her hectically flushed cheeks.

His fingers framed her face. "From the first, desire was there between us. A day will come when the very last word you wish to employ with me is *no*," he declared.

**LYNNE GRAHAM** was born in Ireland and, at the age of fifteen, submitted her first romantic novel, unsuccessfully. Just when she was planning a career, a Christmas visit home resulted in her having to make a choice between career or marriage to a man she had loved since her teens. They live in Ireland in a household overflowing with dogs, plants and books. When their seven-year old daughter was a toddler, Lynne began writing again, this time with success.

# LYNNE GRAHAM

## an arabian courtship

### *Harlequin Books*

TORONTO • NEW YORK • LONDON
AMSTERDAM • PARIS • SYDNEY • HAMBURG
STOCKHOLM • ATHENS • TOKYO • MILAN

For Berta and Michael
With love

Harlequin Presents first edition November 1990
ISBN 0-373-11313-7

Original hardcover edition published in 1989
by Mills & Boon Limited

# CHAPTER ONE

POLLY'S throat constricted when she saw the long limousine turning through the gates of her home. She linked her hands together to stop them trembling. Prince Raschid ibn Saud al Azarin was about to arrive. She turned away from the view.

'Why are you standing over there?' her fifteen-year-old sister demanded. 'You won't be able to see him.'

'I think I can wait for that pleasure,' Polly muttered tightly.

Maggie was swiftly joined by twelve-year-old Joan and four-year-old Elaine, who had not a clue what the excitement was about but was determined not to be left out of it. The window-seat was a tight squeeze for the three of them, each craning their necks for a better view. In an effort to to calm her nerves, Polly breathed in slowly. What her sisters were finding so fascinating was sheer purgatory for her. Could this be real? she asked herself tautly. This was England in the eighties, an era of female liberation. How could she possibly be on the brink of an arranged marriage to a complete stranger? But she was.

'The car's stopping...it's got a little flag on the bonnet. Those must be the colours of the Dhareini royal family.' It was Maggie cheerfully keeping up the running commentary. 'The chauffeur's getting out...oh, he's very dark, he does look foreign...he's opening the rear door...I can see a trouser leg...'

'Oh, for pity's sake, stop it!' The plea broke from Polly on the back of a stifled sob, shocking everybody into silence.

Guiltily biting her lower lip, Maggie watched her sister sink down into one of the shabby nursery armchairs, covering her face briefly with her spread hands.

'He's not wearing robes,' complained Joan.

'Shut up!' Maggie gave her a pointed nudge. 'Polly's not feeling well.'

Joan stared at her eldest sister with unconcealed horror. 'You can't be ill now! Daddy will blow a gasket and Mummy's nearly in orbit as it is!'

'Polly!' cried Maggie suddenly. 'Raschid is gorgeous—I'm not kidding!'

'Prince Raschid,' Joan corrected loftily. 'You can't be too familiar.'

'For heaven's sake, he's going to be our brother-in-law!' Maggie shot back witheringly.

Polly flinched visibly. Her temples were pounding with the nagging beat of a tension that no amount of pain-killers would put to flight. The morning had crawled past. Hardly anybody had talked over the lunch table. Polly hadn't eaten. Her father hadn't eaten either. As if he couldn't stand the look in Polly's helplessly accusing eyes any longer, he had taken himself off to the library even before dessert arrived.

Maggie placed an awkward hand on Polly's taut shoulder. 'He really is scrumptious-looking, honestly he is.'

'Then why can't he buy a wife at home?' Polly spluttered tearfully into her tissue, her nerves taking her over again.

'Scram!' Maggie glowered at Joan and Elaine. 'And don't you dare tell Mother that Polly's crying!'

Irritated by these histrionics, the ever practical and status-conscious Joan frowned. 'What's she got to cry about? She's going to be a princess. I wouldn't cry, I'd be over the moon.'

'Well, isn't it a shame you weren't the eldest?' Maggie threw the door wide.

The door slammed. Ashamed of her over-emotional behaviour, Polly pushed an unsteady hand through the silvery blonde curls falling untidily over her brow and wiped at her wet eyes. 'I still can't believe this is really happening,' she confided stiffly. 'I thought he mightn't turn up.'

'Dad said there was no question that he wouldn't, it being a matter of honour and all that.' Maggie sounded distinctly vague. 'Isn't it strange that we all used to laugh when Dad bored on about the time he saved King Reija's life by stopping a bullet? I mean, if we've heard that story a hundred times, we've heard it a thousand,' she exaggerated. 'And I used to pull your leg something awful about you becoming Wife Number Two... it was a family joke!'

Well, it certainly wasn't a joke now, Polly conceded miserably. Thirty-odd years ago Ernest Barrington had been a youthful diplomat attached to an embassy in one of the Gulf States. During his years in the Middle East he had spent his leave exploring neighbouring countries. On one such trip he had ventured into the wilds of Dharein in Southern Arabia, a country still torn by the fierce feuds of warring tribes and relatively little more civilised than it had been a century earlier. Her father had been taken ill on that particular journey and had sought assistance from a nomadic encampment presided over by Prince Achmed, brother of Dharein's feudal ruler, King Reija.

Fearing for the young Englishman's health, Achmed had taken him to the palace outside Jumani where he had received proper medical attention. There he had recovered his strength, and shortly before his departure he had been honoured by an invitation to join a royal hunting party.

Out in the desert an assassination attempt had been made on his royal host. The details of that shocking episode were somewhat blurred. Polly's father tended to embellish the story year by year, pepping it up to keep it fresh. Shorn of extras, the most basic version ran that, seeing a rifle glinting in the sunlight, Ernest had thrown himself in front of the King and dragged him to the ground, suffering a minor head wound in the process. Overcome by gratitude and a sense of masculine fellowship, King Reija had stated there and then that his firstborn son would marry Ernest Barrington's firstborn daughter.

'Let me tell you, I was pretty taken aback,' Ernest was wont to chuckle at that point in the story. 'I wasn't even married then! But it was obviously the highest honour the King could think to offer. I should add that, since he's highly suspicious of Westerners, it was an even bigger mark of esteem.'

Thus the tale had been told to entertain dinner guests— a rather lighthearted anecdote of exotic climes and a bygone age. Ernest had not met King Reija again. He had retired from the Diplomatic Service as soon as his bachelor uncle died, leaving him a country estate several miles outside Worcester. However, twelve years ago he had chortled when he learnt of Raschid's marriage to Prince Achmed's daughter, Berah. The news had come by way of an elderly diplomat dining with them. Since then the family had often teased Polly about Raschid, reminding her that the Koran permitted a follower of Islam four wives. But never had anybody seen the idea of Polly marrying an Arab prince as anything other than hilariously funny.

Only when their father found himself in serious financial difficulties a month ago had he thought of renewing his acquaintance with King Reija. As Raschid's father was coming to London on a diplomatic visit, Ernest had requested an appointment with him. 'I shall ask him for a loan. I should think he'd be delighted to help,' he had contended confidently. 'I can't understand why I didn't think of this sooner.'

He had duly gone off to keep his appointment at the Dhareini Embassy. Even before he left home the grey anxiety and strain which had marked him for days had been banished by a very characteristic surge of optimism. Since Ernest had long since forgotten his Arabic, King Reija had talked courteously to him through the offices of an interpreter. Family updates had naturally been exchanged. Ernest had cheerfully produced a photograph of the four daughters and infant son he was so proud of possessing. In return his host had informed him that Raschid had been a widower for four years. Berah had died tragically after tripping and falling down a steep staircase. She had been only twenty-six.

'Naturally I offered my condolences... it could never have occurred to me that the old boy could be leading up to making a thirty-five-year-old promise good. But once I was on the spot, as it were, it wasn't that easy to work up to mentioning the loan,' Ernest had confessed. 'You could have knocked me down with a feather when he announced that his conscience had long been troubled by his failure to honour that promise. I lost no time in assuring him that no offence had been caused, but he seemed annoyed at that, so I dropped the subject. Even when he began asking questions about Polly, I still hadn't an idea of what was on his mind.'

Polly had listened, as aghast as her mother initially was, while the older man lumbered at ever slower pace to the climax. 'He told me that it was his dearest wish to see Raschid married again, and then he shook hands with me and the interpreter said, "It is agreed" and I said, "What's agreed?"

'"My son will take your daughter as his bride," came the reply. I was struck dumb!' her father had bleated, mopping at his perspiring brow. 'Then he started talking about the bride price and things just got out of my hands altogether... if they'd ever been in them, for he's a wily old buzzard. Hard to think, though, where there could be any advantage to him in the arrangement. The chap really does take this honour business very, very seriously.'

Surfacing from these unwelcome memories, Polly emitted a choked laugh. 'I was sold! Why did I ever believe that white slavery was a thing of the past? It's a wonder Dad didn't ask for my weight in gold!'

Maggie's eyes were reproachful. 'Polly, that sounds so awful!'

It is awful, Polly reflected bitterly. Why couldn't the King have offered her father a loan? Why had there had to be conditions attached? Even as she thought that, her saner self intervened to point out that her father was in no position to repay a loan.

'Dad said there was no pressure on you and that it was a decision that only you could make. I know—I was listening outside the library door,' Maggie admitted grudgingly. 'He didn't say you had to marry Raschid.'

That he had ever entertained the crazy concept at all, however, had been effective proof of his desperation. Maggie was still at the age where she saw no flaws in her parents. The sad truth was that Ernest Barrington was much too fond of the good things in life and had always lived above his income. Ladybright had been a small and prosperous estate when he inherited it, but the income from the land had never been up to the demands of a large family and a busy social calendar. When the bank had announced their intention to foreclose and force the sale of Ladybright to settle a backlog of mortgage repayments and an enormous overdraft, the accumulated debts of years of extravagance had finally been catching up on their father.

King Reija had stunned her desperate parent with the offer of a huge cash settlement, equal to meeting his debts and securing the family fortunes into the next generation. A drowning man thrown a rope does not hesitate. Polly doubted that her father had objected to the terms once the money was mentioned; he had been dazzled by the miraculous solution to all his problems. Within an hour of his return home, his attitude of apology and bluster had changed into one of determined good cheer.

'I'm not surprised I've taken your breath away, Polly,' he had been saying by then. 'A prince—what's more, a prince who will eventually become a king.'

Her mother had already had the stirrings of dreamy abstraction on her face. Ten minutes later she had whispered reverently, 'My Polly, a princess!'

Anthea Barrington had been in an awed state of ecstasy ever since. Indeed, both of Polly's parents had a remarkable talent for glossing over unpleasant realities. The jaws of the steel trap had closed round Polly slowly but surely. How could she personally sentence her family to poverty? Her mother was no more capable of coping without money than her father was. And what about her sisters and little Timothy, presently building up his bricks at her feet? Could she deny them the secure and comfortable upbringing which she herself had enjoyed when it was within her power to do otherwise?

And for what good reason could she deny her family her help? It was not as though she was sacrificing the chance of a loving marriage at some time in the future. Why shouldn't she marry Raschid and make everyone happy? The man she loved did not love her...at least, not in the right way. Chris Jeffries was very fond of her, but he treated her like a sister.

His parents were neighbours and close family friends. Polly had known Chris since childhood. And that, she had grasped dully, was the problem. Chris thought of himself as the big brother she had never had.

Polly's teenage years had not been painless. She had often turned to Chris for comfort when the going got rough in her own home. A late bloomer, she had been a podgy ugly duckling in her slim and beautiful mother's eyes. She had been further cursed by shyness in a family where only extroverts were admired. Anthea had never been able to hide the fact that quiet, studious Polly was a distinct disappointment as a daughter. A boy-crazy, clothes-mad teenager always on the trot to parties would have delighted her; one who worked hard at school and went off to university intending to train as a librarian had not. Chris, two years her senior and already enrolled in medical school, had been the only person to understand and support Polly's academic aspirations.

Loving Chris had been so easy. If she had a problem he was always ready to listen. From adolescence Polly had innocently assumed that she would eventually marry Chris. When her puppy fat had melted away and she miraculously blossomed into a slender young woman with a cloud of pale hair and flawless features, she had shyly awaited the awakening of Chris's interest in her as a girlfriend. It had never happened, she reflected painfully.

A year ago at her nineteenth birthday party she had been forced to accept that her dreams were that—just dreams. Chris had lightly introduced her to his current girlfriend as 'Polly, my honorary kid sister,' affection and warmth in his manner and no hint of any other form of feeling. She had stopped living in her imagination.

Returning to university, she had sensibly thrown herself into the dating scene that she had scrupulously avoided during her first two terms. But the dates she had since ventured out on had without exception turned into disastrous grappling sessions concluded by resentful and bitter accusations that she was frigid and abnormal. Her efforts to forget Chris had got her nowhere. She still loved him; she was convinced that she would always love him.

Since she would never marry Chris, did it really matter who she married? Reasoning on that coldly practical basis, she had agreed to marry Raschid and solve her family's problems. And once she had agreed, everybody had forgotten the financial bribe and had begun to behave as if she was being singled out for some great honour.

Unfortunately a decision forged in the valiant heat of the moment was tougher to sustain in the hard face of reality. Reality was the arrival of that car outside and the awareness that downstairs was a stranger who was to become her husband, no matter what he was like and no matter how he behaved. She had given her word and she could not go back on it now. Why would she anyway? A spinster in the family would break her mother's heart. It was ironic that for the very first time she was shining like a bright star on her mother's ambitious horizon.

'You're not dressed yet!' Anthea's harassed lament from the door shattered her reverie. 'You can't possibly let Raschid see you looking...'

'The way I usually do?' Polly slotted in drily. 'Well, he might as well see what he's getting, and I'm no fashion-plate.'

'Don't be difficult, darling,' Anthea pleaded, elegantly timeless in her silk suit and pearls. 'You simply must get changed!'

'Where is he?'

'In the library with your father. We discussed the wedding arrangements. St Augustine's of course, but apparently there'll have to be a second ceremony after you fly out to Dharein. We had a very interesting chat before I left them,' she confided with an almost girlish giggle. 'Do you realise that Raschid didn't see his first wife's face until after the wedding? Evidently that's how they do it over there.'

Polly shuddered. She hadn't even met Raschid and already the wedding was fixed! In addition her mother was managing to behave as if this peculiar occasion was quite commonplace. 'It's barbaric!' she protested.

'Now, darling!' Anthea reproved. 'At least he's broken with tradition to come and meet you properly. What may seem strange to us is perfectly normal to him.'

'You think it's normal for a male of thirty-two to let his father pick a foreign bride sight unseen?' Polly exclaimed helplessly. 'You think he's doing me a favour in even coming here?'

'He is a prince, Polly.'

'I don't care!'

'Parents often do know what's best for their children,' Anthea was beginning to sound shrill. 'Remember what your father said—the divorce rate on arranged marriages is very low.'

In receipt of that grim reassurance, Polly was hurried down to her bedroom where the dreaded dress hung on the wardrobe door—powder-pink georgette. She would look like a little girl in a frilly party dress. What flattered Anthea at five foot nine did considerably less for a daughter of five foot one. Outright panic suddenly seethed up inside her. 'I can't go through with this...I can't!' she burst out.

'Of course you're nervous—that's only natural,' Anthea soothed. 'Raschid's bound to be staying for a few days, and you'll get over that silliness. You really don't seem to appreciate how lucky you are.'

'L-lucky?' gasped Polly.

'Any normal girl would be thrilled to be in your position,' Anthea trilled irritably. 'At eighteen I was married and at nineteen I was a mother. Believe me, I was a lot more happy and fulfilled than you've ever been swotting over boring books. When you have your first baby you'll understand exactly what I'm talking about.'

The threat of future offspring turned Polly as white as a sheet. 'A baby?'

'You love children and he doesn't have any. Poor Berah must have been barren,' Anthea remarked cheerfully. 'Raschid's father will be very anxious to see a male grandchild born to ensure the succession. Only think of how proud you'll feel then!'

Her mother was on another plane altogether. Children...intimacy... Polly was feeling physically sick. The prospect of being used to create a baby boom in Dharein did not appeal to her. No wonder King Reija had decided she was suitable! She was one of five children.

'He's wonderfully self-assured for his age, so charming and quite fabulously handsome. One can tell simply by looking at him that he's a prince. He has an air,' Anthea divulged excitedly. 'His manners are exquisite—I was very impressed. When one considers that he wasn't edu- cated over here like his brother Asif, his English is ex- cellent. Not quite colloquial, but...'

The rolling tide of her mother's boundless enthusiasm was suffocating.

'I'll put your hair up—you'll look taller.' Hairpins were thrust in with painful thoroughness. 'He has the most gorgeous blue eyes. Can you believe that?' Anthea gushed. 'I was dying to ask where he got those, but I didn't like to.'

What the heck did Polly care about blue eyes? Her mother had fallen in love with her future son-in-law's status. He could do no wrong. If he'd been a frog, Anthea would have found something generous to say about him. After all, he was a prince, wasn't he?

'I'm so happy for you, so proud.' With swimming eyes Anthea beamed down at her. 'And it's so romantic! Even Princess Diana was an earl's daughter.'

In appalled fascination Polly stared while Anthea dabbed delicately at her eyes with a lace hanky.

'Polly!' Her father's booming call, polished on the hunting field, thundered up the stairs. 'Where the devil are you?'

She could practically hear the tumbril pacing out her steps to the execution block. But when she froze at the top of the stairs, only her father's impatient face greeted her stricken scrutiny.

'Come on . . . come on!' He was all of a fluster, eager to get the introduction over with. That achieved, he could sit back and pretend it was a completely ordinary courtship. Clasping her hand, he spread wide the library door. He was in one of his irrepressible, jovial host moods. 'Polly,' he announced expansively.

Ironically the very first thing Polly noticed about the tall, black-haired male, poised with inhuman calm by the fireplace, was his extraordinary eyes—a clear brilliant blue as glacier-cool as an arctic skyline and as piercing as arrows set ruthlessly on target.

Ernest coughed and bowed out. He nudged her pitilessly over the threshold so that he could close the door behind her. Once she was inside the room, Polly's legs behaved as if they were wedged in solid concrete. She awaited the charm she had been promised, the smooth breaking of the horrible silence. Unable to sustain that hard, penetrating appraisal, she fixed her attention on a vase of flowers slightly to the left of him.

'You cannot be so shy.' The accented drawl was velvet on silk and yet she picked up an edge within it. 'Come here.'

Tensely she edged round a couch. He didn't move forward a helpful inch. What was more, the nearer she got, the bigger he seemed to get. He had to be well over six feet, unusually tall for one of his race.

'Now take your hair down.'

Her lashes fluttered in bemusement. 'M-my h-hair?'

'If it is your desire to become my wife, you must learn that I do not expect my instructions to be questioned,' he drawled. 'When I command, my wife obeys.'

Polly was transfixed to the spot. That cool of absolute conviction carried greater weight than mere arrogance. She flinched when he moved without warning. Long fingers darted down into her hair, and in disbelief she shut her eyes. He was a lunatic, and you didn't argue with lunatics. He was so close she could smell a trace of expensive aftershave overlying the scent of clean, husky male. In other words, he was ten times closer than she wanted him to be. Her bright hair tumbled down to her shoulders, the pins carelessly cast aside.

'You are amazingly obedient.' Abrasion roughened the low-pitched comment.

Reluctantly, fearfully, she looked up. Some treacherously feminine part of her was seized by an almost voyeuristic fascination. He was superbly built, dramatically good-looking. Even Polly would have sneaked a second glance had she seen him somewhere on the street. High cheekbones intensified the aristocratic cast of his features. Sapphire-blue eyes were set beneath flaring dark brows, his pale golden skin stretched over a savagely handsome bone structure. Up close he was simply breathtaking. But in spite of his gravity and the sleek trappings of a sophisticated image, Polly sensed a contradictory dark and compelling animal vibrancy. He had the unstudied allure of a glossy hunting cheetah, naturally beautiful, naturally deadly. He also had a quality of utter stillness which unnerved her. Overpowered, she instinctively retreated a step, steadily tracked by fathomless blue eyes.

His cool, sensual mouth firmed. 'In the circumstances, your timidity seems rather excessive. I value honesty above all other virtues. It would be wiser if you were to behave normally.'

Silence fell.

'You are still very young,' he continued. 'Can you really have reflected upon the kind of life you will lead as my wife?'

Anybody with the brain power of a dormouse would have run a mile the moment they paused to reflect, Polly decided ferociously. Why did she have to stay put? Because, as Maggie had innocently reminded her, this had been her decision. Her lips moved tremulously into a firmer line. 'Of course I've thought it over.'

'You are probably aware that as I handle my country's investment funds, I frequently travel abroad, but as my wife, you will remain in Dharein. You will not accompany me,' he emphasised. 'There you will mix only with your own sex. You will not be able to drive a car. Nor will you be allowed to leave the palace either alone or unveiled. From the hour that I take you as my bride, no other man may look upon you if that is my wish. Within our household we will even eat separately. Perhaps you have heard that certain members of my family are less strict in their observances of these traditions. I am not. I would not wish you to be in ignorance of this fact.'

Ignorance suddenly seemed like bliss. He described an existence beyond the reach of Polly's imagination. Purdah—the segregation of the sexes that resulted in the practice of keeping women in strict seclusion. Sufficiently challenged by the thought of marrying him, all she could produce was a wooden nod.

Audibly he released his breath. 'You cannot have been accustomed to many restrictions. I understand that your parents regularly entertain here.'

'I don't put in much of a presence.' Polly was thinking of her mother's wrath when she had hidden in a landing cupboard at the age of eleven sooner than recite poetry to family friends.

A winged jet brow ascended. 'When I entertain, you will have no choice.'

Her forehead indented. 'But you can't entertain women on their own?'

His brows pleated.

'You just said that I'd never see another man again. I wouldn't be much use as a hostess,' she pointed out flatly.

A disconcerting quirk briefly shifted his unsmiling mouth. 'It is possible that I have been guilty of some exaggeration on that count,' he conceded. 'But you must understand my surprise that a young woman, raised in so free a society, should be willing to enter an arranged marriage. I was concerned that you might have erroneously assumed that your position as my wife would grant you an exciting and glamorous existence.'

'I expect it to be dull.' The impulsive admission just leapt off Polly's tongue. She shrank from the incredulous glitter irradiating his narrowed stare. 'I mean, not dull precisely, but—well, an Arab wife, who has servants and doesn't get out either... well,' she was faltering badly, 'she can't have very much to do with herself.'

'An Arab wife concerns herself with the comfort of her husband,' he intoned coldly.

He was most erratic in his arguments. 'But you said you wouldn't be around much.'

Even white teeth showed in an almost feral slash against his bronzed skin. 'By that I wished to warn you that I will not dance attendance on you.'

But you expect me to dance attendance on you! she thought. He was a male chauvinist pig, an award-winning specimen. He put chauvinism in line with a capital offence. Stonily she studied the carpet. 'Yes.'

'Our alliance will be one of extreme practicality,' he delivered in hard addition. 'I am not of a romantic disposition. I tell you this...'

'You didn't need to. You wouldn't be here if you were romantic,' Polly interrupted thinly. 'I suppose Mother said something which made you worry that I might be suffering from similar delusions. I'm not.'

For a male receiving a reassurance he had surely sought, Raschid looked unrelentingly grim. 'This becomes clear. Then we are of one mind. I will not receive complaints of neglect when I am involved in the business concerns which take up most of my time.'

By the sound of it, if she ran into him once a week she would be doing well. She smiled. 'No, I won't complain.'

'Had I sacked Dharein from border to border, it appears that I could not have found a more conformist and submissive bride,' he declared very softly. 'But I warn you of this now—should we prove incompatible, I will divorce you.'

That was a piece of good news Polly had not even hoped for. How could they be compatible in any field? He intimidated her. A close encounter with an alien would have been less terrifying. The unashamed threat of domestic tyranny echoed in all his stated requirements.

'You have nothing to say to this either?' he prompted in a husky growl. 'You are composed and content with this future?'

'Are you?' Glancing up unwarily, Polly encountered a hypnotically intense stare which burned flags of pink into her fair skin. A curious tightening sensation clenched her somewhere down deep inside. It made her feel very uncomfortable.

A chilling smile slanted his well-shaped mouth. 'Could I be impervious to the allure of such beauty as you possess?'

No doubt this was an example of the charm her mother had mentioned, and it was absolutely meaningless. When Raschid had first seen her in the doorway, neither admiration nor warmth had coloured his impassive appraisal.

'Although I should confess that I am not in accord with the meeting of East and West in marriage,' he added smoothly. 'I will treat you with consideration and respect, but I will not alter my way of life. The adaptation required will, necessarily, be yours alone. I can only accept your word that you feel yourself equal to this challenge.'

Out of the blue the strangest suspicion came to her, infiltrating her self-preoccupation. Could he possibly want her to refuse him? Surely he could not have come here to invite a rejection which would be an intolerable insult to one of his race and status? Polly cast aside that highly unlikely interpretation. A purist might have respected his refusal to offer empty reassurances about their future together. But all he achieved was a deepening of each and every one of Polly's nervous terrors at the picture of herself, marooned in a strange environment, forced to follow foreign customs while at the mercy of a husband who planned to make no allowances for her.

'I'll do my best,' she mumbled, hating him with every fibre of her being for redoubling her fear of the unknown. He defined an existence which chilled her to the marrow.

He studied her downbent head. 'I can ask no more of you. One must hope that the sacrifices entailed are not more than you find the elevation worthy of. Since I have established to my own satisfaction that you fully comprehend the nature of our future relationship, there can be no necessity for a further meeting between us.'

Laser-bright eyes met her startled upward glance in cool challenge.

'But you'll be staying now...for a while?' she queried.

'Unfortunately that will not be possible. Late this evening I am leaving for New York,' he revealed. 'Nor will it suit my schedule to return here again before the wedding.'

Nonchalantly untouched by her dismay that he cherished no plans to stay on as her parents expected, he bent down to enclose lean fingers to her wrist and raise her firmly upright. Her knees were cottonwool supports. Dazedly she watched him clamp a heavy bracelet to her wrist.

'Your betrothal gift,' he explained, answering her blank stare.

Of beaten gold and studded with precious stones, it was decorated with some primitive form of hiero-glyphics. Polly was put grotesquely in mind of a slave manacle. Valiantly she tried to express gratitude.

A cool hand pressed up her chin, enforcing contact with black-lashed eyes of lapis lazuli which were daunt-ingly enigmatic. Raschid ran the forefinger of his other hand very lightly along the smooth curve of her jawbone, silently studying her, and somehow, while he maintained that magnetic reconnaissance, she could not move. A peculiar disorientation swept her with light-headedness. He dropped his hand almost amusedly. 'I think you will be very responsive in my bed, Polly. I also suspect that you may find your training as a librarian of small ad-vantage to you there. But I await enlightenment with immense impatience...'

Had the door not opened, framing her parents' anxious faces, Polly would have fled there and then. A deep crimson had banished her pallor. Raschid turned to them with a brilliant smile. 'Your daughter is all that I was promised—a pearl beyond price,' he murmured smoothly. 'Truly I am blessed that I may claim so perfect a bride.'

# CHAPTER TWO

THE ORGAN played Purcell as Polly came down the aisle, parchment-pale, her screened gaze avoiding the tall, exquisitely dressed male watching her with untraditional cool from the altar. Throughout the past fortnight of hectic preparations she had existed in a dream state, her brain protectively hung in an emotional vacuum. That was the only way she had coped.

Her mind shifted inexorably back to her parents' dismay when they had realised that Raschid was not remaining with them as a house guest. She had hoped ... what had she hoped for? Dismay had swiftly become acceptance. In awe of him, her parents had put up no objections. They were not even attending the second ceremony in Dharein. From the moment Polly left the church she would be on her own.

At the altar she received a wide smile from the smaller, younger man to Raschid's right—presumably his brother Asif. Reddening, she dropped her head and the vicar's voice droned on in her ears. Beside her lounged a primitive male, who regarded her solely as a piece of sexual merchandise he had bought off a shelf. Involuntarily she shivered. Raschid had made it brutally clear that she would have no place in his life beyond the bedroom door. Her blood had run cold under the intensely sexual slide of those assessing eyes, the appraisal of a natural-born predator.

They were on the church steps when she saw Chris. As he waved, her shuttered face came alive. It was three months since their last meeting. Raw and seething bitterness surged up inside her. It should have been Chris beside her posing for the camera . . . it should have been Chris inside the church. The ceremony she had just undergone was a mockery. Without hesitation she hurried down the steps towards the slim, fair-haired man smiling at her.

'Aunt Janice said you mightn't be able to come,' she murmured tightly.

Chris laughed. 'Wild horses wouldn't have kept me from your wedding! You look stunning.' Grasping both her hands, he looked her over and grinned. 'What happened to your ambition to be a career woman?'

'You tell me.' Responding to his easy smile took all her concentration as she fought back stinging tears. She was embarrassed by her adolescently eager dash to his side, but the familiar sight of him had drawn her instantly.

'Hey,' he scolded, and the underlying seriousness of his gaze deepened, 'the bride's not supposed to cry! Whirlwind romance or not, I hope he's the right man for you. You deserve the best.'

Polly's throat closed over. The truth of what lay behind her sudden marriage would have appalled him, yet pride kept her silent. What more proof did she require of his indifference to her as a woman? He would dance at her wedding with a light heart. He had never realised how she felt about him, and now he never would. 'I wouldn't have settled for less.' Her over-bright smile stretched to include Asif as he approached them.

'Sorry, I have to kidnap the bride. The photographer's fuming,' he explained in a clipped Oxbridge accent.

'Oh, lord, I forgot about him!' Polly gasped.

He steered her away, lustrous dark eyes skimming her guilty face, his appreciative grin widening. 'Is there anything else that you forgot? Like a new husband? If you'll forgive me for saying so, it's not terribly tactful to go surging at ex-boyfriends with Raschid around—unless you have a death wish, of course. But I'll grant you one point. You staggered him—a rare sight to be savoured.'

Reluctantly Polly met Raschid's veiled gaze a moment later. 'I'm sorry,' she lied.

He cast her a grim glance. 'You don't appear to know how to behave in public,' he drawled in an icy undertone that flicked down her spine like the gypsy's warning. 'But you will be taught, of that I assure you.'

In angry disbelief, still trembling from the force of her disturbed emotions, she flared, 'Who the blazes do you...?'

His jawline clenched. 'I will not tolerate disrespect from you!'

Gritting her teeth, Polly spun to walk away again. The long-suffering photographer had finished. Raschid's hand closed round hers, denying escape, but she broke her fingers violently free, muttering bitterly, 'Tell me, what do you do when you're not bullying women half your size? Beat them? I'd sooner know now!'

The blaze of fury that silvered his gaze shook her rigid. Had they not been surrounded by people she had the certain knowledge that she would have discovered exactly what Raschid did for an encore. Guiltily conscious that hating him for not being Chris was irrational and inexcusable, she retreated hastily.

'Lordy, what sparked that off?' Maggie whispered.

'An unholy temper that I never suspected he had.' Polly stole a driven glance over her shoulder to check that she hadn't been followed. A choking sense of trapped misery enfolded her.

She should have apologised on the drive back to the reception at Ladybright, but she didn't. Like an over-shaken bottle of Coke, she was afraid to uncap her sealed lips lest she explode. Her nerves were jangling a dangerous discordancy. Seeing Chris, so near yet so far, had agonised her, and her self-discipline was threatening to crumble.

Over the meal she did her utmost to ignore Raschid.
The tension zapped in the air like static electricity. Unable
to face food, she knocked back the champagne. She
didn't even notice how much she was drinking. When
everybody began circulating, Polly, who was normally
retiring in company, was suddenly to be seen speaking
personally to every guest present. Absently marvelling
that she no longer felt like throwing herself under a bus,
she laughed at another one of Chris's medical jokes,
frowning when Maggie pulled at her sleeve.

'You have to get changed.' Maggie hustled her determinedly out of the room. 'What on earth are you playing
at? You're sozzled! Mother hasn't even realised—she's
busy telling everybody what wonderful confidence a
woman gains from getting married.'

Polly gripped the banister and pronounced with
dignity, 'I have never taken alcohol to ex—excesh in my
life.'

'That's why it's gone straight to your head. How could
you be so stupid?' wailed Maggie. 'Even I can see that
Raschid doesn't like it. Didn't you notice that he hasn't
touched a drop? He's not knocking it back like his
brother. This just isn't like you!'

'But I'm a confident married woman now.' Polly
pirouetted and nearly tripped over her train, remaining
dizzily still long enough for Maggie to detach her veil.
'I shall stand up for myself. I won't be bullied!'

'How about strangled?' her sister groaned, struggling
to unzip her. 'Sometimes you are a klutz, Polly. When
Raschid saw you in the church he couldn't take his eyes
off you—and no wonder, you looked ravishing! But now
he looks...well, if I were you, I'd eat humble pie.'

'Rubbish—start as you mean to go on,' Polly overruled as if her craven evasiveness had been the first step
in a deliberate offensive.

'And as for the way Chris kept on following you
about...'

'Any reason why he shouldn't have?' snapped Polly, turning her head away. When would she ever see Chris again? If she had made the best of a last opportunity to be with him, who could blame her?

Maggie frowned uncomfortably. 'He couldn't take his eyes off you either. I've never seen Chris act like that with you before.'

Polly hadn't noticed anything. An insane thought occurred to her. Wouldn't it be simply hysterical if Chris had finally appreciated that she was a woman and not a sister the day she married someone else? Macabre and unlikely, she decided bitterly.

Attired in her elegant going-away outfit, she was propelled out on to the landing to throw her bouquet. She peered down at all the upturned faces and swayed, dropping the bouquet in their general direction. Negotiating the stairs rivalled coming down an escalator the wrong way. On the bottom step she lurched, and strong arms came out of nowhere and caught her.

'Whoops!' she giggled, clashing accidentally with sapphire eyes that emanated all the warmth of an icebox. 'Go on the wagon,' she mumbled as if she was making a New Year resolution, the remainder of her alcohol-induced euphoria draining away. 'Promish.'

The hiccups started on the way to the airport. Clapping a hand to her mouth in horror, she tried to hold them in. It was about then that she began to notice the silence. By the time she was steered into the opulent cabin of the private jet, she was sending Raschid's hard-edged profile unwittingly pleading glances. The derisive charge of the look she received nearly pushed her over the edge into tears. She fumbled for the right words of apology for her outburst on the church steps. After take-off, she voiced them hesitantly.

Raschid leant forward without warning and snapped hard fingers round her narrow wrists to yank her up to face him. 'You are drunk!' he raked down at her in disgust.

'T-tiddly,' Polly corrected unsteadily, moisture shimmering in her unhappy eyes.

His contempt unconcealed, he released her to sink back white and shaken into her seat. She mumbled another apology, shrinking from the shamed awareness that he was right. But just for a while, under the influence of Dutch courage, her fear of him had vanished. Now it was returning in full force, stronger than ever before.

'Silence!' he cut across her stumbling apology. 'Was it not shame enough that I must accept a bride who sells herself for money like a vendor sells his wares in the street? But that you should dare to turn up at that church and then make an exhibition of yourself as my wife is intolerable!'

'I'm sorry!' she sobbed again.

'I told you to keep quiet,' he lashed icily down at her. 'I may have been deceived, but it is you who will suffer for it. After the brazen behaviour I witnessed today, you will find yourself confined to the palace!'

'I wasn't going to get out anyway!' Polly wept all the harder while he towered over her like a hanging judge pronouncing sentence.

'I will not acknowledge you publicly as my wife until you learn how to conduct yourself like a lady, and I have never seen anything less ladylike than your display this afternoon!'

The harsh condemnation genuinely shattered her. Without warning all the dammed-up tensions and resentments she had been forced by family indifference to suppress exploded from her. Her head flew back. 'I...hate...you!' she launched. 'Don't you dare insult me. I did my best. I even tried to hide the fact that if it wasn't for the money, I wouldn't have married you if you'd been the very last man alive! And if you don't want me either, I'm just delighted about it! Do you hear me? You're a domineering, insensitive tyrant, and I shall get down on my knees and beg your father to deport me. No wonder he had to come to England to find you a wife . . . no wonder!'

During her impassioned tirade, Raschid had frozen. He could not have been more astonished by the diatribe had a chair lifted on its own steam and begun a physical assault on him.

Curled up in a tight ball, Polly squinted up at him through tear-clogged lashes. 'No woman with an IQ above forty would want to marry you and clank about in chains for the rest of her days, trying not to show how h happy she is when you're thousands of miles away . . .'

'I believe it is time that you were sobered up.' He bent down, and Polly was off that seat so fast with a piercing scream that she caught him totally by surprise. Having read brutal retribution into that grim announcement of intent, she lost what control remained to her and squirmed along to the far corner of the couch, tugging off a shoe in the blind, terror-stricken belief that she required a defensive weapon.

The cabin door burst wide, the steward and stewardess rushing in. Polly was quite beyond the reach of embarrassment. Stark fear had her cowering, tears pouring down her cheeks in rivulets.

A dark bar of colour overlaid Raschid's hard cheekbones. He spoke at length in Arabic and then quietly dismissed their audience. A hand plucked the raised shoe from her stranglehold and tossed it aside. 'I would not offer a woman violence,' he ground out with hauteur.

'I'm numb, I won't feel it,' she mumbled incoherently.

A pair of arms firmly scooped her drooping body off the seat. 'You will feel calmer when you have rested.'

He carried her into the sleeping compartment, settling her down with unexpected care on the built-in bed. Tugging off her stray shoe, he calmly turned her over to unzip her dress. Cooler air washed her spine. In dismay she attempted to escape his attentions, as he glowered down at her. 'Do you really think that I could be tempted to seize you passionately into my arms at this moment? A hysterical child does not awaken desire within me.'

Having decimated the opposition, he seated himself to divest her smoothly of her dress. Leaving her clad in her slip, he pulled the slippery sheet over her trembling length. Already dazedly recovering from the kind of scene she had never before indulged in, Polly was gripped by remorse. Not only had she affronted him before the cabin staff, she had been unjust. Her resentment would have been more fairly aimed at her parents for cheerfully letting her enter this marriage and blithely ignoring reality.

Could she really even blame them? The pressure on her had been enormous, but she had agreed to marry Raschid. Unfortunately there was a vast gulf between weak resolution and her feelings now that she was on the spot. She swallowed chokily. 'I don't know what came over me . . . I . . .'

The steady beat of his gaze was unremitting. 'There is nothing to explain. You were afraid—I should have seen that fear and made allowances for it. But I too have feelings, Polly,' he delivered with level emphasis. 'Financial greed may be permissible in a mistress; it is not in a wife. For that reason I have given you little cause to rejoice in the bargain.'

There was something about him in that instant, some deep and fierce emotion behind the icy dignity and hauteur. For the very first time, Polly suffered a driving need to know how he felt. Bitter? Disillusioned? His anger was gone. What she sensed now, she could not name, but it sent a sharp pang of pain winging through her.

She didn't want to talk about the money. She couldn't face the reawakening of the chilling distaste he had shown earlier. What would be the point of it? The money lay between them and it could not be removed. But for the money she would not be here. Raschid despised her for her willingness to marry him on that basis alone. The whys and wherefores didn't abate his harsh judgement. And the revelation that she loved another man would scarcely improve his opinion of her. Suddenly more ashamed than ever, she whispered, 'I didn't mean what I said.'

An ebony brow elevated. 'I am not a fool, but I ask you this—if that is how you feel, why did you marry me?'

She could not bring herself to play the martyr, pleading her family's need as excuse. Absorbing her unease in the tortured silence, he sighed. Brown fingers brushed a silvery pale tendril of hair back from her warm forehead. 'I had reason,' he said softly. 'To look at you gave me pleasure, and in spite of what you say to the contrary, I could put your aversion to flight so quickly that your head would spin . . . for when you look at me, Polly, you desire me.'

'That's not true!' Her hostility sprang immediately back to the fore.

The tip of his forefinger skidded languidly along the fullness of her lower lip. His eyes had a richly amused glint now. 'True, my little Polly,' he contradicted.

Her mind was a blank. She was shaken by her sudden explosive physical awareness of him. His sexual impact that close was like a punch in the stomach, yet she did not retreat from it. 'You're not angry any more,' she muttered.

'Be grateful for your visual compensations. I learnt long ago that the perfection Allah denies in the copying of nature is no more easily to be found in human beings, especially in those of your sex,' he stated quietly. 'The inviting smile which falsely offers tenderness and understanding—that I do not require from you. You will be as you are with me. That I will respect.'

He slid fluidly upright. 'We will forget today. I don't believe you knew what you were doing. Had that been obvious to me, I would not have spoken so harshly.'

Reeling from that imperturbable calm and gravity, Polly was agonisingly conscious of the seismic force of the personality behind the cool front. He had not once lost control. She had behaved appallingly, but he had remained cool-headed enough to see her hysteria for what it was. While grateful for his calm, she squirmed from the lash of his superior perception.

A knock sounded on the door. 'That will be the meal I requested. You ate very little earlier,' he reminded her. 'I also ordered a restorative drink for you—before we parted Asif assured me that it was an infallible cure for a hangover. Drink it and then sleep.'

Disconcerted yet again, Polly couldn't even look at him. The stewardess entered, darting a nervous glance at Raschid, who appeared to figure in her mind as a wife beater. Guilty pink suffused Polly's cheeks. He had treated her with a kindness few men would have employed in the circumstances. Dully she reviewed the reckless, thoughtless immaturity of her own showing throughout the day. The contrast did not lift her spirits.

She was wonderfully relaxed when she woke up. Only as she shifted and came into startling contact with a hair-roughened thigh did she realise where she was, and her eyes flew wide.

'Good morning.' Raschid leant up on his elbow. Reading her shock, he laughed. He looked ruffled and in need of a shave and unnervingly, undeniably gorgeous. Black hair, golden skin, blue eyes—a devastating combination. Smiling, he moved a hand lazily and tugged a strand of her hair. 'Come back over here. Or do I have to fetch you?'

'F-fetch me?' she quavered.

He snaked out his hand and settled it on her slim waist, his fingers splaying to her hipbone to propel her coolly back towards him.

'No!' she gasped in alarm.

'Yes.'

'No... I'm not joking!' she cried feverishly.

Raschid laced his other hand into the tangle of her hair and held her frightened green eyes steadily. 'Neither am I, Polly.' He pulled her the last few inches, sealing her into union with his long, hard length. 'And there is nothing to fear, only much to discover,' he promised huskily.

Her hand braced against a sleek brown shoulder, only to leap quickly away again. His dark head bent, the brilliance of his eyes somehow sentencing her to stillness. Taking his time, he brushed her lips with his, and she trembled, lying as rigid as a stone statue in his embrace. He strung a line of light, butterfly kisses over the arc of her extended throat, softly, sensuously dipping a smooth passage across the delicate tracery of her collarbone while his fingers skimmed caressingly over the sensitive skin of her back.

Polly's limbs turned fluid without her knowledge. A strange heat blossomed in her pelvis. She quivered as his palm curved to the swell of her hip and he moved sinuously against her, teaching her the depth of his arousal and momentarily shocking her back into tension. He nuzzled at the tender expanse below her ear and her cheek curved into the pillow, her body awash with fluttering sensations which completely controlled her. With a soft laugh, he finally returned to her mouth, playfully coaxing, introducing her to the myriad textures of his firm lips and sharp teeth and the velvety roughness of his tongue, until the blood drummed in her veins with burning excitement.

Catherine wheels and shooting stars illuminated the darkness of her mind. It was everything she had ever secretly dreamt of, everything she had never expected to feel, except...except... The thought eluded her. Raschid's hands traced the shape of her breasts with erotic mastery, moulding, stroking, inciting. A tiny moan escaped her. A searing rush of almost painful pleasure arched her body up into the heat and potency of the all-male body over hers. Then as suddenly she was freed.

Her glazed scrutiny rested on her treacherous fingers. Anchored in the springy vitality of his hair, they prevented him from further retreat. Strickenly she retrieved them.

He skated a mocking fingertip over her ripe mouth, his eyes bright pools of incredible blue, tautness etched over his flushed cheekbones. 'I am very tempted to enjoy the delights of the bridal chamber with you now.' Straightening with an earthy groan, he looked intently down at her. 'However, that would not be wise. But at least you may now appreciate that you need have no fear of me tonight.'

Pushing back the sheet, he slid out of bed, not a self-conscious bone in a single line of his lean, sunbronzed body. Tonight. A blush warmed what felt like every inch of her skin. She had lain there and actually let him...at no stage had she objected. But on a level with that shockingly polished technique of his, her experience was nil. Raschid could not be compared to the teenage boys, full of selfish impatience, who had grabbed her roughly, attempting to infuse her with a matching passion, only to fail. Never once had she understood what she was supposed to feel during those embarrassing sessions.

Now, in the arms of a male who was virtually a stranger, she found out, and she was in shock. Had he been Chris she would not have been surprised. But he wasn't Chris and he wasn't remotely like Chris. Nor could she ever recall yearning for Chris to touch her.

That accidental acknowledgement slid in and jolted her. It was true, she realised in bewilderment. Picturing herself drifting from the altar with Chris, she had then seen them in a dozen cosy settings, but never in one that centred on sexual intimacy. Something in her retreated uneasily from an image of Chris as a lover. Confused by the awareness, she buried it. Hadn't she seen friends succumb to dangerous physical infatuations that burnt out through the lack of any more lasting fuel? Her feelings for Chris had always seemed infinitely superior. She had felt safe. She knew better, she had thought.

And Raschid taught her differently. Carelessly, easily, with the light touch and control of an expert lover, he had showed her what physical hunger was—a wanting, unreasoning ache without conscience, powerful enough to destroy every scruple. She was disgusted with herself. And dear heaven, he was like Jekyll and Hyde! Whatever she might have expected, it had not been that heart-stoppingly sensual persuasion which had effortlessly overcome her resistance. He bewildered her.

He had calmly referred to the wedding night still to come. Panic reclaimed her. What had she done in marrying him? Suddenly she was waking up to the full portent of what marrying Raschid entailed. How could she go through with it? How could she actually go to bed with a stranger? She was not some medieval maiden raised to be bartered in matrimony. Environment had not conditioned Polly to submissively accept her fate without argument.

She was sitting up when Raschid reappeared from the shower-room, towelling his hair dry. Crimsoning at the amount of masculine flesh on view, Polly lost inches of recaptured poise and studied the bed. 'We need to talk,' she muttered.

'I am here.'

Nervously she breathed in. 'Earlier you seemed to make it pretty clear that I couldn't be the sort of wife you want.' She paused. 'Maybe you'd prefer to call a halt now.'

'A halt?'

'An annulment.'

An unexpected laugh greeted her stilted suggestion. 'I presume you are trying to amuse me?'

Indignantly she glanced up. He looked totally unfamiliar in flowing robes of soft cream. 'Actually I'm being constructive,' she told him.

'Don't you think your desire to be—constructive,' he repeated the word very drily, 'is a little late?'

Polly bit her lip. The suggestion had been born of cowardly impulse. Undoubtedly it must seem to him as if she wanted to renege on the agreement after having collected the profits. 'But you said you wouldn't acknowledge me,' she protested lamely.

'I too may say things in anger which I do not mean. I seriously doubt that you have a drink problem, and even if you had,' his beautifully shaped mouth slanted expressively, 'you are unlikely to find any outlet for it in Dharein.'

'I don't understand you!' Frustration rose in her.

'Our meetings to date have not encouraged either of us to behave naturally,' he returned with infuriating composure. 'And to talk of annulment now when we are married is really quite ridiculous.'

Defensively she stiffened. 'That's the only time you *could* talk about annulment...you don't give a damn how I feel, do you?'

He viewed her narrowly. 'You would like me to be honest? I came to your home with no idea of what reception awaited me there. I cherished no inclination to marry any woman.'

'I beg your pardon?' she cut in.

'I believe you heard me, Polly. Nor can I accept that this news surprises you.'

Hearing was not always believing. He had not wanted to marry her. The information stung and shocked like a sudden slap on the face. A deep sense of incredulous mortification crept over her. 'Then why did you come?' she asked.

'In the hope that you might withdraw as I could not.' Raschid dealt her an unrelentingly sardonic glance, his mouth cynically set. 'But that hope was swiftly laid to rest, wasn't it? However I might have behaved, my proposal would have been acceptable to you and your family. But I am not one to quarrel with what cannot be altered. You are beautiful. *Insh'allah*. It could have been worse.'

As she listened with a slowly dropping jaw, a tide of rage unfettered by reasoning even of the meanest form was building inside her. 'How could you marry me thinking like that? It could have been worse,' she parroted in enraged repetition. 'And how...dare...you get into bed with me!'

Raschid bound a gold *agal* round his headress. 'There may be a certain piquancy to our mutual reservations, but they are unlikely to spill over into the marital bed. There you do not find my attentions offensive.'

'Don't you dare throw that at me now! I had no idea what you were thinking then!' she rebutted stridently.

'I have explained my feelings to you.' The inflection was one of definite reproof, clipped and controlled. 'Now I suggest you dress suitably for your audience with my father. We will be landing soon.'

Sudden moisture gritted her eyelids and she blinked, her anger deflated. Raschid was gone, and she was unutterably crushed by what he had coolly dropped on her. The black joke of the century was on them both. Prince Raschid ibn Saud al Azarin had not wanted to marry her either. Damn him to hell! she thought abruptly. If that was true, why were they here now? Why had he even come to Ladybright? Oh, she wanted to scream! Some outdated code of honour had made him come, had made him refrain from admitting his unwillingness. But now—when he told her it was too late—he had slung it at her with hauteur, as if Polly and her family had gone in pursuit of him with a shotgun. Now she could review his grim and guarded manner at their first encounter. She had fallen hook, line and sinker for an act. The arrogant swine had actually been trying to put her off!

Equating his arrival with unquestioning acceptance of the marriage, she had been too wrapped up in her own anxieties to appraise his attitude logically. But why had he gone through with it? Her thoughts chased in concentric circles, her temper rising afresh. He had the gall to inform her bluntly that her sole saving grace was her face and figure. Suddenly she was dismissed as an individual and reduced to the level of a sexual plaything. It could have been worse—indeed? If it crossed her mind that there was a strong hint of the biter bit in her enraged reaction, she refused to identify it.

'The obvious solution is a divorce as soon as possible,' she pronounced, entering the cabin, her slender curves fetchingly attired in a full-length pale green gown which accentuated her air of spun silver delicacy.

'Don't be a child, Polly.' Raschid glanced up from the papers he was studying at his desk, awarding her reappearance the most cursory interest.

She folded her arms, wrathful at being ignored. 'If the only thing that brought you to Ladybright was that stupid assassination attempt on your father and the crazy promise he made then, I'm not being childish.'

Blue-black lashes swept up like silk fans. 'I cannot refrain from saying that the attempt might have ended in a death which would have been tragic for my country's survival and stability,' he replied abrasively. 'But I will concede that I too consider that promise to be rather... odd. My father is not a man of ill-judged impulse.'

'But, like him, you believe in this honour nonsense.'

'A concept which few of your sex have the unselfishness to hold in esteem. The pursuit of the principle infrequently leads down a self-chosen path,' he delivered crushingly. 'Nor was I made aware of the pledge between our fathers until three weeks ago.'

Polly was astonished. 'Only three weeks ago?'

'There was no reason for me to be told sooner. When I married at twenty, you were still a child. Since my father could not have supposed that an Englishwoman would desire to enter a polygamous marriage——' He paused. 'Although having met you and your family, I would not be so sure.'

It took her a minute to unmask that base insult. She flushed to the roots of her hairline while he spoke on in the same coolly measured tone.

'My father cannot always have believed in that promise to the degree which he presently contends. Had it been otherwise, I would have been informed of it years ago,' he asserted. 'But I understand his motivation and I speak of it now, for it is no secret within the palace. It has long been my father's aim to force me into marriage again.'

# CHAPTER THREE

STUNNED by the unemotionally couched admission, Polly sank down on the other side of the desk. 'But why me, if he didn't believe . . . force?' she queried.

'The promise supplied the pressure. The means by which my father attained this conclusion might not be passed by the over-scrupulous.' Raschid smiled grimly. 'But be assured that before he even met your father, he would have made exhaustive enquiries as to your character and reputation.'

'I was investigated?'

'Without a doubt. You are very naïve, Polly. You cannot suppose that my father would have risked presenting me with a bride likely to shame or scandalise the family.' Sardonic amusement brightened his clear gaze.

In retrospect it did seem very foolish of all of them to have believed that King Reija would gaily give consent to his son's marriage to a woman of whom he knew nothing. Raschid's revelations put an entirely different complexion on her father's meeting with him in London. Assured of her unblemished reputation and goodness knew what else, Raschid's father had calmly manipulated hers at the interview. From the outset he must have known of her father's debts. They could not have escaped detection.

Too much was bombarding Polly too quickly. The amount of Machiavellian intrigue afoot even between father and son dismayed her. But why had coercion in the form of that promise been required to push Raschid into marriage? While he might still grieve for Berah and appear virtually indifferent to her successor's identity,

40

he did not strike her as impractical. His position demanded that he marry and father children; that responsibility was inextricably woven into his future as a
duty. Could he be so insensible to the necessity?

'I don't understand—you don't really seem angry with
your father,' she said.

'I must respect the sincerity of his intentions. He truly
believes that a man without a wife cannot be content.
In his view a married man is also a respectable and stable
man,' he volunteered, an inescapable harshness
roughening his intonation.

'But why didn't you want to remarry?' Polly pierced
to the heart of the matter, weary of skating round the
edges.

'I preferred my freedom,' he breathed dismissively.
'Since I had spent most of my adult life married, what
else?'

'Well, if you're so darned keen to have your freedom
back, I'm not holding you!' Polly sprang furiously
upright.

'Why this sudden alteration in attitude?' Raschid
studied her quizzically. 'What has changed between us
except a basic understanding? We stand at no different
level now from that we stood at within that church.'

Anger shuddered tempestuously through her. 'Yet
somehow you're behaving as if I trapped you into
marriage!'

'Nobody traps me, least of all a woman. I made a
decision. If I had to remarry to satisfy my father's expectations, why not you?' he traded softly.

'I notice too that, while your father mysteriously
emerges from all this as morally above reproach when
he's been wheeling and dealing like the Godfather, I'm
still being insulted!'

'How have I insulted you?' He vented a harsh impre-
cation. 'I thought you would be quiet and inoffensive,

but the second you left that church you suddenly located a tongue!'

Admittedly Polly had had difficulty in recognising herself over the past twenty-four hours, but the most even temperament would have been inflamed by Raschid. 'Blame your father. Obviously he didn't dig deep enough,' she sniped, nettled by his candid admission that he had deemed her the type to melt mutely into the woodwork. 'I find you unbelievably insensitive!'

'And I find you like every other woman I have met in recent years—demanding.' Exasperation laced his striking features. 'Were you so sensitive in marrying a stranger purely for his wealth?'

Already very pale, she cringed from the cruel reminder. Pride made her voice the comeback, tilting her chin. 'Was that how you viewed your first wife as well?'

He was very still. In the dragging quiet, her heart thudded loudly in her eardrums. The fierce chill of his appraisal forced colour up beneath her skin. 'There can be no comparison. Berah grew up knowing that she would become my wife. Nor was she unaware of the nature of the man she was marrying. You know nothing whatsoever about me.'

Her stricken eyes fell from his. While her reference to Berah had been foolish, she had not been prepared for the charged and telling force of Raschid's defence of her. His fingers were rigidly braced on the edge of the desk. The comparison she had dared to suggest had deeply angered him.

'I don't think you're being very fair,' she argued. 'And I'm not demanding.'

A lean brown hand shifted abruptly. 'Let us have no further arguments. On this subject they lead nowhere.'

'What subject? What are we arguing about? I don't know.'

He lounged indolently back. 'Really?' A dubious brow quirked. 'In the space of an hour you refer to annulment and divorce. This is not, after all, some form of attention-seeking?' he derided. 'You want pretences—compliments, gallantry, romance. I disdain all of those, and I won't play charades. I employed candour with you before today. We each had our price in this marriage. Mine was peace and yours was status and money. Now that that is established, what more can there be worthy of debate?'

'I can tell you right now,' Polly slammed back shakily for want of any other brickbat to hurl. 'Being a princess is not all it's made out to be!'

'You may tell me whatever you wish if you reward me with a still tongue and the sound of sweet silence.'

She retreated to the opposite end of the cabin. He had gone over her like an armoured tank and the track marks of the vanquished were on her back. She had reacted emotionally to a male who did not allow emotion to cloud his reasoning. Or his judgement. He thought that she should have left her family to sink in the horrors of bankruptcy rather than sell herself into marriage. He was delicate in his sensibilities—he could afford to be. Bitterly Polly appraised the outright luxury of her surroundings. Without money her family would have fallen apart. Neither of her parents would have had the resilience to pick themselves up and soldier on.

Yet for all his contempt now, Raschid had been remarkably tolerant about a wedding which could have made a hit disaster movie. In bed—she reddened hotly at the recollection—he had been teasing and warm. But both responses had been logically perfect for the occasion. You didn't calm a hysteric with threats. You didn't coax a frightened virgin with force. Not unless you were stupid, and Raschid, she was learning by painful and clumsy steps, was far from stupid. He was dauntingly clever and dismayingly complex.

Abstractedly she watched him. Even in violent resentment she remained disturbingly conscious of the dark vibrancy of his potent attraction. In combination with looks and wealth that blazing physical magnetism of his must have stopped many women in their tracks. Polly had always distrusted handsome men; they were normally chockful of vanity. Raschid's distinct lack of self-awareness puzzled her. He was stunning, but she had the strangest suspicion that the only time he looked in the mirror was to shave.

Abruptly she denied her view of him by removing to a poorer vantage point. She couldn't understand what was wrong with her. Even when the stewardess served her with a meal, her thoughts marched on. Raschid was beginning to obsess her even as his emotional detachment chilled her. Linked with that raw, overt masculinity of his, that coolness made him an intriguing paradox.

Why had he been so reluctant to remarry? There could only be one reason: a reluctance to set another woman in Berah's place. But Polly found it hard to attribute the longevity of passionate love beyond death and sentimental scruples to that diamond-cutting intellect. What other reason could there be? Accepting that he had to remarry, he had settled for Polly. He liked looking at her; he didn't like listening to her. Then he wouldn't have to listen much, would he? Not with the workload and the travel itinerary he had bent over backwards to outline.

The jet landed with a nasty judder, careening along the runway, the nearest porthole displaying a blur of what looked like desert. Assuming that the airport was oddly sited somewhere out of view, Polly got up. Raschid presented her with a bundle of black cloth. Her blank appraisal roused his impatience. Retrieving it, he shook it out and dropped it over her startled head.

'I can't breathe!' she protested.

'Don't be ridiculous!' Light appeared as he adjusted the set of the suffocating garment. Disorientatingly, he burst out laughing. 'You look very strange, Polly. This *aba* was not cut for someone of your height.'

Yanking up the surplus fabric, she stalked after him. Just outside the doorway, as she was interestedly taking in the sight of a line-up of soldiers and the presence of a small military band, striking up the most unmelodic tune she had ever heard, her foot caught in the hem of the *aba*. Hearing her gasp, Raschid whirled with incredible speed. As she teetered she was abruptly snatched off her feet and pierced by blazing blue eyes. 'You are the most extraordinarily clumsy female I have ever come across!'

'I wasn't planning on wearing a shroud until I went to my coffin!' she snapped back.

His sudden pallor did not escape her. Too late did she understand the source of his wrath. But before sympathy could touch her normally generous heart, outrage took over. Dear heaven, was Berah never out of his thoughts? Here he was carting Polly home, and all she could think about was his first wife!

'Put me down, please,' she demanded icily.

'It's only a few steps to the car.' Indeed it was, and after throwing the unfortunate band an unappreciative glance, he stuffed her inside the limousine like a parcel. In bewilderment she stared out at the huge grey fortress walls rising to sheer heights with no perceivable end only a few hundred yards away.

'Where's the airport?' she queried.

'That is the palace. A jet-strip was built here for convenience. The airport is on the other side of Jumani.'

'That's the city?'

'I am overwhelmed by the interest you have taken in your future home.' His scorn for her ignorance was unhidden. 'Jumani is ten kilometres from here.'

In embarrassment Polly turned to peer out at the gigantic nothingness of the desert terrain stretching in all other directions. It went on into infinity to meet the colourless vault of the sky, a wasteland of emptiness and rolling hills of sand. The isolation was indescribably alien to visual senses trained on green fields and hedgerows.

The limousine whisked them over to the black, shimmering ribbon of road and through the gates of the palace into a vast, cobbled courtyard. Already the heat was making Polly's clothing stick to her damp skin. Raschid's door sprang open immediately. He stepped out to be met by a spate of Arabic from the little man bobbing and dipping rather nervously in front of him. He frowned and swept off.

When he halted as if he had forgotten something ten yards on, Polly just wanted to kick him for striding back to haul her out of her death struggle with the *aba* twisted round her legs. 'That is not a very graceful fashion in which to descend from a car,' Raschid commented drily.

He guided her through the crush emerging from the great domed porch ahead. Glimpsing dark faces and avidly inquisitive female stares, she was ironically relieved to be covered from head to toe.

'I understand that my father wishes to receive us immediately,' he explained flatly. 'You will not speak—I don't trust you to speak lest you offend. On unfamiliar ground I do not believe you are at your most intelligent.'

Burning inside like a bushfire, Polly bit down hard on her tongue. He stopped before a set of carved double doors which were thrown wide by the fearsome armed guards on either side. He strode ahead of her. At a reluctant pace, she followed, to watch him fall down gracefully on his knees and touch his forehead to the carpet. For seventy, the grey-bearded old gentleman seated on a shallow dais at the foot of the room looked admirably hale and hearty. Polly got down on the carpet just as Raschid was signalled up. The King snapped his fingers and barked something in Arabic.

Raschid audibly released his breath. 'Get up.'

Before she could guess his intention, he had deftly whipped the *aba* off again. Polly felt like a piece of plundered booty, tumbled out on the carpet for examination and curiously naked under the onslaught of shrewd dark eyes. Reija passed some remark, chuckled and went on to speak at considerable length. Turning pink, Polly slowly sank down again, but not before she noticed the rush of blood to Raschid's cheekbones. Whatever his father was saying to him was having the most extraordinarily visible effect on him. His knuckles showed white as his hand clenched by his side. A pin-dropping silence stretched long after King Reija had finished speaking.

Suddenly Raschid spat a response. Polly was shocked. A split second later a wall-shaking argument was taking place over her averted head. Father and son set into each other with a ferocity which would have transcended any language barrier. The silences, spiced by what could only be described as Reija's inflammatory and self-satisfied smiles, grew longer. Abruptly Raschid inclined his head and backed out. Polly nervously looked up again.

A gnarled hand beckoned her closer. 'A most unfortunate introduction to our household,' said Reija in heavily accented English. Noting her surprise, he smiled with distinct amusement. 'I speak your language. However, it has often been of great benefit for me to listen rather than to converse.'

Somehow Polly managed a polite smile. Her gormless father had not had a chance against that level of subtle calculation!

'You are welcome,' he pronounced. 'Such pale beauty as yours can only draw my son more frequently to his home.'

It wasn't her place to tell him that he was in for a swift disillusionment. Raschid was about as adapted to having his wings clipped as a bird of prey deprived of a kill. But it was interesting to learn that his father wanted to see him here more often than he evidently did. Reassuring too, she conceded absently. Arguments between father and son were seemingly not evidence of some deep schism in their relationship. Yet she was frustrated by her inability to understand exactly what was going on around her. What had incited Raschid to barely leashed rage and roused his father to only sardonic amusement loudly voiced?

'A man does not drink brackish water when he may sip sweetly within his own household.'

Bemusedly Polly blinked, having been briefly lost in her own thoughts. Fortunately a reply did not seem to be expected.

'It is my hope that you will soon come to consider our country as your home.'

She gulped. 'Yes.'

'To facilitate this you will wish to learn Arabic.' He nodded to himself. 'A tutor will be found for you.'

At least he didn't talk in riddles. She was King Reija's gift to his son—unfortunately bestowed upon an ungrateful recipient. But that, she suspected, was most unlikely to keep the King awake at night. He looked mighty pleased with himself. The same steely obstinacy and ingrained ruthlessness that distinguished the son was reflected in the father.

'Your father—he is well?'

'Yes, Your Majesty.'

'May he live long and prosper.' He waved a hand. 'You may withdraw—the women are impatient to prepare you for the wedding.'

When Polly emerged Raschid searched her eyes almost fiercely. What had caused that argument? she questioned frustratedly. It had driven Raschid into his current dark, smouldering mood. For all his outer detachment, he seethed with intense emotion just beneath the surface.

'He suggested that I learn Arabic.' In an effort to dispel the tension she smiled.

His jawline hardened. 'Do not make that effort for my benefit. It is not important to me,' he asserted harshly.

All over again Polly experienced that lowering sense of rejection. This time, however, she controlled her anger. Reality had finally sunk in. She could evade it no longer. This arrogant, unfathomable male was her husband. If they were at daggers drawn now, it was her own fault; her foolish references to annulment and divorce must have taxed his patience to the limits. She had spouted hot air. Her pride had smarted under a candour that had only equalled her own.

Breathlessly she hurried to keep up with his long stride. He led her down a bewildering succession of corridors. The palace complex was vast, composed of a hotch-potch of two- and three-storey buildings, many of them fashioned round traditional inner courtyards, the various wings linked by passageways and staircases. She would need a map and a compass to get round on her own. As the thick walls echoed with their footsteps, she thought anxiously about the womenfolk awaiting her, glad that her father had been able to fill her in on the distaff side of the family.

King Reija had married three times. His first wife had died in childbirth. His second, Nurbah, was Raschid and Asif's mother. For years she had suffered from a heart condition that had sentenced her to an invalid's existence. Perhaps that was why her husband had chosen to marry again. His third wife, Muscar, had had a daughter, Jezra, who was now sixteen. That alliance had ended in divorce, although Jezra remained within her father's household.

Apart from Jezra, there was Asif's wife, Chassa. She was the mother of two baby girls, and she was only twenty-two. Polly had tried not to look aghast when her father had added that Chassa was expecting yet again, no doubt in pursuit of the baby boy without which no Arab husband could be satisfied.

Shying away from the too intimate tenor of her reflections, she glanced at Raschid and reddened. 'What did you and your father argue about?'

'That is not open to discussion. Suffice it to say that my father and I do not always share the same sense of humour.' His expressive mouth tightened.

Annoyed by the curt brush-off, she said, 'I don't think I want to marry you again. Once was enough!'

He cast her a predatory half-smile. 'But I wouldn't dream of depriving you of the excitements of an Islamic wedding. To deny that to one who, not two short weeks ago, expressed her willingness to live as I live would be inconceivably cruel,' he murmured with silken satire.

Polly trembled with indignation. Raschid mounted a marble staircase slightly ahead of her and then hung back for her to catch up. He was thinking about 'her' again. It was a wonder he hadn't thrown himself into the grave with her. Polly frowned, shaken by the meanness of the thought and the quite unjustifiable annoyance from which it had sprung. Berah had died suddenly, tragically. What kind of man would he be if he did not remember?

At the head of the staircase he stilled. 'I must leave you here. You will find my sister through that door to your left.' His gleaming scrutiny lingered impenetrably on her. Before she could turn away he reached out a hand. 'But first,' he said huskily, drawing her inexorably closer and lifting a hand to lace long fingers with unnerving slowness into the tumbled fall of her hair, 'this.'

In the shadows of the wall he captured her lips urgently. 'Open your mouth,' he demanded, his breath fanning her cheek, and then his tongue hungrily plundered the intimacy she had denied him.

It was as if the ground fell away from beneath her feet. Her hands clutched at his shoulders for support. She had no control over the surge of hunger that sent a scorching flame to the very centre of her body. It controlled her. Raschid controlled her. In instinctive repulsion, Polly jerked her head back, devastated by the immediacy of her response to him.

'You are quite right.' His eyes were veiled, his mouth taut. 'I forgot myself. This is not the place.'

'I don't think anywhere's the place. If this is a marriage of convenience, why do we...?' She swallowed, apprehensively measuring the midnight blue flare of his gaze. 'You know what I'm saying.'

A winged brow elevated. 'I don't need to justify myself, Polly. Remember that tonight. Patience is not one of my virtues. You chose this,' he drawled with ruthless emphasis.

She whirled away from him through the door he had indicated. Finding herself under the questioning appraisal of a tall, rather plump girl with a strong resemblance to Asif, she blushed.

'You must be Jezra.' Polly summoned up a self-conscious smile.

Jezra pointedly ignored her extended hand. Her rounded face was sullenly stiff, her brown eyes cold. 'I will take you to your maids. Zenobia speaks English, Gada none. But I doubt if you'll be here long enough to improve anyone's vocabulary!'

'I sincerely hope you're right.' As soon as the words left her, Polly regretted them, but she was mentally and physically exhausted. Jezra's hostility, following so fast on Raschid's coldly implacable insistence that she share his bed, was the last straw. 'Look,' she added hurriedly, 'I'm rather tired. Can we begin again?'

Mottled pink had highlighted Jezra's complexion. 'Raschid didn't even want to marry you!' she spat.

'Jezra, please——' Polly began heavily, but the tirade was unstoppable.

'Why should he have? His mistress in Paris, she is twice as beautiful as you—tall and blonde. I hear the men turn in the street to watch her go past. No matter what our father believes, you will not supplant her!' Suddenly the teenager fell silent, her eyes appalled.

Polly had lost every scrap of natural colour.

'It was a lie, a wicked untruth,' Jezra muttered frantically. 'You mustn't repeat it to Raschid.'

The rich blend of colours in the carpet blurred under Polly's strained gaze. 'I've no intention of repeating it to anyone.'

The intense silence throbbed. Jezra cleared her throat. 'I must ask you to forgive me for the rudeness of my welcome.'

She was very pale now, obviously frightened. Polly might have felt sorry for her had she not felt sorrier for herself. 'It's forgotten,' she said flatly.

The final piece of the jigsaw puzzle slid into place, the unknown factor which had evaded her. At last she had a more practical explanation for Raschid's aversion to remarriage. Small wonder that he was content as he was and his puritanical father had put on the pressure to return his son to a more respectable path. Bile soured Polly's throat. King Reija had supplied Raschid with a blonde on the home front, as if blondes were interchangeable—and maybe they were on Raschid's terms. He did not intend to deny himself the self-indulgence of making love to his bride. Jezra's revelation rocked Polly to her foundations.

The teenager showed her through to an elegantly furnished bedroom. A pair of smiling young girls moved forward. A spill of gorgeous fabric lay across the divan bed. Her wedding outfit? Polly looked bitterly away.

She was a pawn on a chessboard here in Dharein. To think that she had actually felt ashamed of her inability to enter this marriage with dignity and acceptance: Her misgivings now had concrete proof. Raschid planned to use her as a front for some sordid affair. It was a dirty, devious, dishonourable piece of skulduggery. Chris would never have done this to any woman. Chris was honest and decent.

Locked in her despondency, she quietly let Zenobia help her undress. She slipped gratefully into the cool of a cotton wrap and was guided through to the connecting bathroom before she realised what was intended. Gada was sprinkling aromatic perfume into the water already awaiting her.

'I really don't need a bath,' she said stiffly.

'It will be most refreshing, I promise you.' Zenobia's tiny hands sketched an almost pleading gesture. 'We must wait upon you, *lellah*. Have we displeased you?'

It was easier to submit than to argue. When Raschid lay ahead of her, all else had to pale into insignificance. Her hair was washed five times, left with the texture of oiled silk. Stepping from the bath, she was wrapped in velvety towels. While she lay face down on a divan being gently massaged with rose-scented oil by Zenobia, her heavy eyelids drooped. She slept, awakening with a timeless sense of dislocation. Gada was expertly employing a fine brush to paint delicate henna swirls on her hands and feet. Polly tried politely to object, but ran aground on Zenobia's anxious explanation that this procedure was the custom for the bride.

A chattering cluster of women awaited them back in the bedroom. Jezra stood sulkily off to one side. It was ritual, Polly realised grimly, all of it, from the minute she had got into the bath—hours of age-old ritual to ready the bride for her lord and master. Three elderly women were squatting in the corner chanting what sounded like a funeral dirge. Uneasily averting her eyes, Polly stood while her audience communicated in dumb show.

'Do any of them speak English?' she asked.

'These are Bedouin, *lellah*. They are the women of Queen Nurbah's tribe,' Zenobia explained. 'Very few of them come into the town, but it is tradition that they dress Prince Raschid's bride. They are honoured to be accepted by you as attendants.'

In any other situation Polly would have found the friendly atmosphere contagious, but the strangeness of it all made it another endurance test. She had no idea what they did to her face; there was no mirror in view. She was assisted into the sumptuous silver and blue kaftan. A swathe of crimson silk covered her hair turban fashion and a headdress of beaten silver coins was attached low over her forehead. Only then was she allowed to approach a mirror. A shimmering bejewelled odalisque met her dazed scrutiny. Polly Barrington had vanished.

She was escorted downstairs to Queen Nurbah's apartments, the women following but remaining outside. Raschid's mother was reclining on a daybed, her lined features bearing witness to her poor health.

'I am sorry that I cannot rise to greet you.' Warmth in her creased eyes, she held out a beringed hand for Polly to kiss. 'My doctor insists that I am excluded from the festivities. I am very disappointed. Jezra, the girdle is on the bed. You must perform this service for me.'

Kneeling, Jezra linked a silver belt round Polly's hips and fastened the teardrop sapphire clasp. The women outside stretched out reverent fingers to touch the girdle. At Polly's enquiring glance, Jezra averted her head. 'It is a symbol of fertility,' she explained, surprisingly embarrassed.

Zenobia attached the veil to Polly's face and the procession passed on. In a chamber dimly lit against the darkness now beyond the windows, Raschid awaited her, a tall, still figure, magnificent in dark blue silk robes. His sapphire eyes began at the top of her head and roamed intently down over her. He didn't smile. Whether or not he found it amusing that she should be presented to him as a glittering Arab bridal doll was unrevealed by the impassivity of his bronzed features.

The ceremony was short, witnessed by King Reija and several other solemn-faced men. Hot with mortification, Polly stumbled over every Arabic phrase she had to repeat. Her hand was bound in a length of green cloth attached to Raschid's wrist and released again. She was then hustled back to the door, suddenly alarmingly conscious of Raschid's gleaming gaze following her. Loathing stabbed rawly into her. Consideration and respect didn't cover a mistress.

In a large reception room full of women, a slim, graceful girl with almond-shaped eyes moved to greet her. 'I am Chassa.' She leant forward to kiss Polly's cheek. 'I hope we shall be friends. Don't worry about names, but you must meet everyone.'

After a giddy surge of introductions, an array of colourful dishes were brought to her and the celebrations got under way. Voices, clattering dishes and music reverberated painfully against the headache Polly was developing. She could not get a morsel of food past her sore throat. Chassa sat beside her. She had attended an English boarding school and, optimistically in search of a common acquaintance, she named almost every girl she had met there. Polly struggled to ward off the nagging tiredness which made her feel as if Chassa was talking to her through a glass wall.

At some stage of the endless evening Zenobia touched her shoulder to indicate that she must now leave. Chassa gave her a teasing smile. Polly's spirits sank to her toes. Her stomach turned over sickly. She was borne off by a bunch of bustling matrons on a long trek through shadowy passageways and up a wide staircase to be thrust into an enormous room, dominated by an equally enormous and ornately carved four-poster bed. A wave of giddiness passed over her as the door slammed loudly on the ladies' exuberant departure.

# CHAPTER FOUR

HER apprehension of some ghastly form of medieval bedding ceremony removed, Polly breathed again. A carved wooden frieze did justice here as a window. The shutters were drawn back and beyond the frieze swam the milky globe of the moon in violet-hued heavens. Unaffected by the night's beauty, Polly shivered convulsively. A breeze filmed over her damp skin, the chill matching that in her veins. Within these walls the twentieth century seemed a cruel illusion. She had been delivered like a gaudily wrapped present for her new husband to unwrap.

Shakily she trailed off the veil and the headdress. A cloud of musky fragrance was released into the air as she shook out her confined hair. Her temples were throbbing now, and she grimaced. She refused to go through with the rest of this charade. How could Raschid seriously expect her to? At the sound of the door opening, she spun violently, her heart in her mouth.

His luxuriant black hair uncovered, Raschid now wore only a light cream robe. As he approached her, a faint smile softened his firm mouth. His eyes glittered over her. None of her fearful tension was mirrored in his relaxed bearing.

'I am relieved that you didn't undress completely and get into bed to await me,' he mocked, cool palms resting on her shoulders as he studied her with contrasting sombreness. 'You are my wife now.'

Polly's brain was woolly, her head was starting to spin. Dimly she grasped that there was something more than nerves amiss with her. Only willpower enabled her to force the weakness back and stand straight. 'I can't get into that bed with you!' she blurted out.

He dropped down fluidly on one knee and unclasped the girdle. 'I will carry you there,' he promised, snapping free the first of the countless silver buttons, beginning at the very hem of her kaftan.

'I can manage those for myself,' she muttered, stricken by his lack of reaction to her controversial announcement.

Unexpectedly throaty laughter shook him. A hand halted her retreat, tugging her firmly back within reach. 'The hundred and one buttons are mine to undo. With each I glimpse another...' He surveyed her in sudden reflective silence. 'A most provocative custom,' he completed gently.

'For a man,' she interposed tremulously. 'If you think that I intend to stand here while you strip me...'

The lean brown fingers did not hesitate at their self-appointed task. 'This I do not think—I know,' he countered with perfect cool. 'You are nervous, Polly, but you are my wife.'

The repetition of that brutal fact slid through her unnaturally taut figure. Abandon hope, all ye who enter here, she reflected crazily. His wife. All individuality, all rights of self-determination wrested from her by a single ceremony. 'This...this is barbaric!' she whispered.

'Think before you speak. I will not endure insults tonight.' Hard warning chased the previous huskiness from his deep, dark drawl.

Shivering, Polly crossed her hands over her breasts. 'You're not being very...reasonable, Raschid.' Her wide eyes implored his understanding. 'We're strangers! I can't just...'

Rising soundlessly, he uncrossed her defensive hands, his gaze silvery and unyielding. 'You entered this marriage of your own volition, aware that this moment would arrive.'

Oxygen locked in her aching throat. 'I didn't think about it . . . I couldn't!'

'You will not refuse me.'

'I'm not refusing. I . . . I . . .' She faltered to a halt, not really knowing what she was saying but overpoweringly aware of the charge of anger her objections were unleashing in him. He hadn't raised his voice; he didn't need to. The atmosphere was dry as tinder ready to burst into crackling flames.

'I find this emotional display offensive.'

'I expect you would,' Polly muttered helplessly. 'It's not a problem you're likely to suffer from, is it?'

Raschid's hand closed over her wrist, yanking her back from the further retreat she had been unconsciously making. 'You are my bride. What you seek to deny me is no longer yours to deny,' he asserted icily.

She trembled. 'That's medieval!'

'Be careful you do not discover just how medieval I can be.' He sounded the threat with syllabic sibilance, his nostrils flared, his golden features ruthlessly cast. In his proud demeanour he was every inch a barbaric desert prince, the fierce and pagan image of a feudal culture in which it was unthinkable for a wife to disobey her husband. 'You make an impressive start to our marriage, do you not? For what, after all, did you offer me on our first encounter but this?'

Her fingers pressed to the annoying pulse flickering wildly at the base of her throat. The aggression she had incited utterly intimidated her and she felt incredibly weak. 'That isn't the way it was.'

'How was it?' Derision brought violet brilliance to his challenging stare. 'Did you offer me intelligent conversation? Did you try in any fashion to impress me except as a beautiful woman?'

Polly winced from the lash of his contempt. 'I was nervous . . . embarrassed. I didn't know what to say to you.'

'Yet you cared not what awaited you. You cared only that I took you. You did not even ask me if you would be my only wife,' he reminded her. 'And I told you then that I would bed you.'

'Don't you dare talk to me like that!' She backed to the corner of the bed, her hand clutching at one of the posts for support. She was tempted to throw her knowledge of his mistress at him but too afraid of sending his temper right over the edge. 'Don't you realise how I feel? All you see is . . .'

'My bride defying me, and I do not like it,' he incised succinctly.

'All you see is an object. Don't you think I have feelings?'

An imperious brow lifted. 'Do you consider mine?'

'You have none.' She leant back breathlessly while he calmly continued to flick loose the buttons. She did not even have the energy to put up a token fight. 'A wedding ring,' she whispered bitterly, 'does not dignify lust.'

The metallic sheen of Raschid's suddenly savage scrutiny made her quail. She loosed a gasp of fear as he moved and swept her up to tumble her down on the bed. 'With that charge on our wedding night you insult me beyond belief. I have tolerated much from you since we left that church; I will tolerate no more.' His intonation was raw. 'I bought you. I own you. That is the pact which you made.'

Shattered, she stared up at him. He met her shocked eyes levelly. The declaration had not been made for effect. *I own you.* Her whole being recoiled from that primal affirmation of possession. As the canopy above her seemed to be revolving, she pushed her hands down on the mattress to lift herself up. The motion took enormous effort of will. She was so cold now that her teeth wanted to chatter. Her silence appeared to have defused his anger.

He came down beside her, reaching up to dim the wall lights before gathering her into his arms. 'Polly, let us not begin in discord and bitterness. You should not fear what is natural between a man and a woman.'

A draining tide of dizziness tipped her head back, the argent fall of her hair tumbling over his arm. His voice was coming and going like a buzz-saw in her ears.

'Raschid,' she framed hoarsely.

'Listen to me.' His natural assurance emerged even in the low pitch of his roughened murmur. 'It is desire which burns in me. That is not lust. There is no giving in lust—it takes and despoils. That is not how I would initiate my bride into the pleasures of lovemaking.'

Her eyes slid shut as his fingers rested against her cheek. He said something harsh in Arabic, his hand skimming up to her brow, but Polly was already becoming limp, slipping without argument down into the emptiness of oblivion.

'Awake?' A thermometer was thrust in her parched mouth. A strange and yet somehow familiar face, thin and topped by a frilly green hat which contrasted violently with the carrot-red hair, swam into clarity above her. 'Do you know where you are today? Not to worry, you're over the worst. It's not often I've seen that high a fever with influenza.' The stark Glaswegian accent increased Polly's sense of unreality.

Out came the thermometer at last. Polly tried to move, and discovered her limbs were weighted. Her body was weak as a kitten's. Lethargically she turned her muzzy head. Sunlight was casting lacy shadows through the frieze on to the Persian carpet on the floor. Everywhere she looked, flowers flourished in a riot of colour. Dust motes danced in the air. Her attention wandered back to the nurse. 'How do you come to be here?' She winced at the corncrake rasp of her voice.

'Noticed I'm not a local, have you? Then you're well on the mend. I'm Susan MacKenzie.' An almost depressingly cheerful grin came her way. 'I'm on contract with the Jumani City Hospital. I was brought to the palace on the first night, along with every consultant in the building.' She laughed uproariously at the recollection. 'Half the palace inhabitants were crammed outside that door. You didn't half create a panic!'

Polly grew even paler. 'What day is it?'

'Saturday. You couldn't possibly remember much. You've been out of your skull and wandering ever since you became ill. It's a marvel that nobody realised that you weren't well. Still, 'flu can take you very suddenly, and with all that make-up you had on, they couldn't have told just by looking. Talk about the gilded lily!'

Polly's sluggish brain edged back to the wedding and the wedding night. Embarrassment swallowed her alive. By the sound of it, she had given Raschid the kind of night he would never forget! A dramatic collapse on the marital bed seemed a fitting end to a disastrous wedding. Tears lashed her eyelids, but she was too weak to shed them.

'You must be gasping to see your husband,' Susan MacKenzie burbled. 'It might be a while before he appears. Until your fever broke last night he hardly left this room. He's probably sleeping now—he must be exhausted.'

Polly closed her aching eyes. She had made a thorough nuisance of herself. What choice had Raschid had but to play the devoted new husband? And if the tender trap of marriage had inspired him with aversion, the reality of it within days must have left him gnashing his teeth.

An hour later, washed, brushed and nearly deafened by Susan's endless chatter, she was having chicken broth spooned into her. After a nap, she wakened to find Jezra seated by the bed. The teenager immediately grasped her hand fervently, her swollen eyes swimming with tears.

'I am so glad that you are getting better, Polly. Even if Raschid never forgives me for the cruel words I spoke to you in anger, I am glad. Please believe me. I am so glad,' she sobbed, emotion overcoming her.

Polly was soon patting her shoulder and doing her best to soothe the distressed girl. Her illness had infused Jezra with the guilty and superstitious conviction that her revelation had somehow taken its toll. Firmly telling her that that was nonsense, Polly prompted, 'How did Raschid find out about it? Susan said I was rambling. I hope I didn't . . .'

'I told him. My conscience troubled me,' Jezra whispered. 'He was very angry, and who could blame him? What will I do if he tells our father?'

The unlikelihood of that event curled Polly's mouth. 'I shouldn't worry about that.'

Jezra sighed unhappily and fiddled with her tissue. 'I repeated a dreadful slander. I am ashamed to admit that I believed in it. Now I know how wrong I was to listen to gossip. Raschid is not like that.'

While remaining cynically unconvinced of Raschid's sainthood, Polly smiled reassuringly in the hope that the mortifying topic might be killed between them for good. Perceptibly Jezra brightened. 'It wasn't that I didn't like you, I didn't know you, but Raschid was so unhappy with Berah,' she volunteered in a rush. 'I was afraid that you would make him unhappy as well.'

Her lashes concealing her perplexity, Polly took a charged breath. Raschid's sister was patently unaware that she might be telling her something which she didn't already know.

'All she could think about was babies. All she could do was cry and be depressed,' Jezra muttered scornfully. 'I am sure you are different. My brother is a very fine man.'

The facts had been staring her in the face. She had been too dumb to see the obvious. How could Raschid's first marriage have been happy? A childless marriage in an Arab society where sons were so highly prized as proof of a man's virility could not have been blissfully content. If Berah had not adapted to her infertility, the relationship must have been a severe strain on Raschid as well. But he must have loved her, he must have loved her deeply not to divorce her or take another wife. In his position there could be no other explanation.

When the door opened both their heads spun. Jezra took one look at the motionless figure on the threshold and got up, scuttling out past her elder brother with alacrity. Had Polly had the power of her legs and the innocence to believe she could manage a similar exit, she would have copied her.

Painful heat washed her cheeks. Raschid had never seemed less approachable; his bright eyes were guarded, his expression sombre. 'I am relieved to see you so much improved. Your health has been a matter of grave concern to all of us.'

She bent her head, overtly conscious of the wan and thinned reflection Susan MacKenzie had shown her in her hand mirror. She looked ghastly. And if even she, who had never had much interest in her appearance, thought that, how much worse must she look to him? 'I'm sorry,' she said. 'I've caused a lot of trouble.'

He expelled his breath. 'Is this how I appear to you— as a man who expects his sick wife to apologise for the impossible? I am not such a man. If I were to tax you with any failing—and this must be said in case you are equally foolish on some future occasion—why didn't you tell me how you were feeling?'

With hindsight Polly realised that she had gone through the wedding in an increasingly feverish haze. Until the artificial stimulants of tension and self-discipline had come crashing down inevitably in this same room, she hadn't realised how very ill she was feeling.

Awkwardly she endeavoured to explain that to him, her fingers restlessly creasing at a corner of the white sheet.

'You were burning up when I touched you. You must have known that you were ill.' Raschid sighed heavily. 'When you fainted I felt very little different from a man bent upon rape.'

At this startling admission her head flew up.

'I am not so insensitive that I would make sexual demands of a sick woman, whatever you may believe me capable of,' he stressed in a taut undertone.

She evaded his unusually expressive eyes. Reproach was unhidden there. 'I didn't believe that,' she muttered. 'I didn't think...'

From somewhere surfaced the memory of those eyes above hers when she was ill. Beautiful, compelling eyes which had inspired her with oddly lyrical and sentimental comparisons. As it occurred to her that she might have spoken them out loud, she was ready to crawl beneath the sheet. Of course, she'd been delirious. Undoubtedly she had talked senseless gibberish.

Raschid took the seat his sister had vacated. He was very constrained, his smile remarkable only in its brevity. 'I sometimes believe that you think very infrequently where I am concerned—but we need not talk of that night again,' he declared. 'You were clearly not in full possession of your senses. I do not hold you responsible for what you said then.'

A grin suddenly threatened the tight line of her mouth. Hurriedly she squashed it. He looked so deadly serious. He was proffering what she estimated to be on his terms a forgiveness of the utmost generosity. Lunacy must have been upon her—how otherwise would she have dared to fight with him? But perhaps only now did she comprehend how very deeply she had offended him that night.

'We have a great deal to discuss.'

Polly tensed, recoiling from the threat of Raschid openly raising the subject of his mistress and telling her the same lies that he had evidently told his trusting sister.

'However, some matters are better postponed until you are stronger,' he decreed.

He was letting the dust settle on Jezra's inopportune bombshell. A splendid move from a skilled diplomat, Polly realised with bitter resentment. By the time he did raise the subject, the immediacy of drama would be long gone, and in his mind, leaving himself currently undefended was probably as good as a declaration of innocence. It would take some early bird to catch him out!

A lean hand enclosed hers, spinning her out of her fierce introspection. 'I always seem to be approaching you with criticism,' he said.

'I expect you believe that you've had cause.' Polly was in no mood to think guiltily of their catastrophic wedding and its equally trying aftermath from his point of view. That short-lived generosity had steadily receded from her.

'No. It is this failing I have of making assumptions, of jumping the...' He hesitated.

'Gun?' she filled in shakily, outrageously conscious of the thumb absently caressing the tender skin of her inner wrist.

He frowned. 'Why didn't you explain to me that your father was in debt? I had no knowledge of the fact. Your family appeared to be living in comfort and prosperity.'

Polly blinked. 'You didn't know about Dad?'

'When I visited your home I knew nothing about your family. Now I suspect that the bride price went to your father and not to you. Is this not true?' he prompted. 'You gave the money to him?'

Polly didn't recall having anything to actually give. She had a vague memory of signing some papers at her father's request. 'I suppose so, but what...?'

'I understood that the money went solely to you.'

'Me?' she echoed, finally picking up his drift. 'Good lord, what would I have done with it?'

A less guarded smile curved his well-shaped mouth. 'I believed that you became a woman of financial substance by our marriage. In short, I believed that you had married me for your own enrichment, encouraged to that move by your parents. Instead I now learn...'

'How did you?' she interrupted.

'You were most talkative in your fever,' he breathed, abruptly releasing her thin fingers.

She flushed at the confirmation. 'It's not really important now, is it?'

Rising from the chair with the natural grace that accompanied all his movements, Raschid had strolled over to the window. She was surprised that he should turn his back on her; it was a gesture considered very rude by his race. But as she spoke, he immediately turned, presenting his hard-edged profile to her. 'On the contrary,' he murmured quietly, 'I now perceive you as you are. You didn't marry me for personal gain, you obviously did so for your family's benefit. Naturally this must alter my view of you, and you may not wish to hear me say it, but I think very ill of parents able to smile so happily while they barter their unwilling daughter into marriage with a stranger.'

'It wasn't like that,' Polly muttered.

He sent her a winging glance. 'You forget—I was there. Had I been less prejudiced against you, I would have suspected the true circumstances sooner. Your behaviour was self-explanatory. It was your parents who forced you to the match.'

'I made the decision,' she insisted.

'I disagree.' The contradiction was coolly emphatic. 'When one makes a decision one accepts it. To say the very least, you were not in a state of acceptance when you married me.'

Unsure where this was leading, Polly said nothing. In any case, he had spoken the truth. Depressed about Chris and deeply concerned for her family, she had plunged into giving her consent. She had not thought the decision through, she had run away from it. In confusion she appreciated that Chris had not entered her head until Raschid had put him there by association. Recalling her torment at the wedding, she wondered where all that emotion had gone. It did not hurt now. Why? Why didn't it hurt?

Raschid sighed. 'All you must concentrate on now is recovering your strength. I have stayed too long. That dreadfully garrulous woman will assault my ears. Is she ever silent?' he enquired wryly.

She gave him an absent glance. 'No, but she's kind. I like her.'

'Then the purpose was fulfilled. I thought you would be happier with a British nurse.'

'Thank you for the flowers,' she whispered shyly before he reached the door. 'They're beautiful . . . nobody's ever given me flowers before.'

Chris slipped out of her puzzled musings and her lashes drooped on the flower-bedecked room and the not very cheerful reflection that the floral offerings were worth about as much as the statutory visit Raschid had made. He could not be seen to neglect an ailing wife.

'Only twelve weeks to Christmas, but who would credit it?' Susan MacKenzie stared out unappreciatively at the sun slowly sinking in a blazing glory of crimson and cerise and peach before she returned to brushing Polly's hair. 'I can't wait to get home and be cold and get wrapped up in woollens. Will you miss Christmas?'

Polly's eyes watered. 'Yes.'

'Smile!' hectored Susan. 'You're almost on your feet again. You're suffering from the post-flu blues, that's all. It's only ten days since you were really ill. Then I know you're fed up with this room. That's why you're getting a surprise.'

Polly had had more surprises than she could handle over the last week. Raschid four or five times a day had been a big enough shock to her expectations. Sometimes he stayed only a few minutes, other times he stayed an hour. He never came empty-handed. The bedside cabinet was piled high with paperbacks. If he didn't bring books, he brought flowers or magazines. But half the time he was there, he was broodingly silent, forcing Polly to chatter nervously non-stop.

An intense cloak of reserve characterised Raschid. She could never tell what he was thinking. He had a trick of listening with acute interest no matter what trivial rubbish she was spouting. It had to be a very useful device when he was caught up in boring business meetings, but Polly found it frankly unnerving.

His body language was far from informative. He never relaxed in her company. He paced restlessly like a prowling cheetah confined in a too small cage. He also maintained a distance from the bed that suggested he was in the presence of dangerous contagion.

Polly had gone over and over their conversation ten days earlier, searching for the source of his constraint and his avoidance of the tiniest show of intimacy. But she was essentially in the dark as to the cause. She did suspect that the knowledge that she had succumbed to outside pressures in marrying him had ironically flicked Raschid's pride on the raw. He might have assured her that he now saw her differently, shorn of her brazen guise as a weak-hearted gold-digger, but why did she receive the peculiar impression that a money-grabbing blonde would have been more welcome to him? She frowned. That was just another in a long list of imponderables, and Raschid was full of them.

'You're not very curious, are you?' Susan rattled on. 'Don't you want to know what the surprise is? You're dining with your husband tonight!'

Instead of reacting in blushing confusion, Polly paled. Why on earth would he make such an effort? Guilt? He was leaving for New York again tomorrow. No doubt he was breaking his neck to engage in a passionate reunion with his mistress. He probably had no trouble at all in talking to her. Maybe she even travelled with him. Suddenly her eyes misted with tears and she bent her head quickly over a letter from her sister. It was the 'flu which was making her miserable, wasn't it? She was fed up with herself. These moody highs and lows of temperament were unfamiliar to her.

Maggie had mentioned that Chris had spent the weekend at Ladybright. Polly sighed and set the letter down. Thoughts that would have been heresy to her a month ago had been bombarding her increasingly of late, and she knew why. Her devastating physical response to Raschid had pointed out a glaring lack in her feelings for Chris, forcing her to question them. How could she love Chris without ever having longed to physically express that love? Yet, incredibly, that was what she had done for the past four years.

Had she mistaken liking and admiration and loneliness for loving? The idea that she could have so misunderstood her own emotions dismayed her. But what else was she to believe?

She had missed Chris terribly when he started medical school. She had been hurt and lost as their childhood closeness stretched to a more adult gulf. But those were growing pains, weren't they? Chris had been mature for his age, while she hadn't been, she acknowledged ruefully. A shy, introverted teenager, she had depended heavily on Chris as a friend. Had she stubbornly clung to an adolescent dream longer than other girls?

The lingering remnants of that rosy dream world had died on her wedding day. Of course it had hurt, even though her love for Chris had been a highly idealised and quite impractical thing. In a sense it had been a security blanket as well while no one else attracted her. And all this time she had really cared for Chris as he cared for her. If it had been real love she would not have been defenceless against Raschid.

When Raschid came in she was reading. Glued to the printed page, she didn't hear him. 'Is that enthralling?' he queried.

Glancing up, she did a forgivable double-take. Raschid was wearing an open-necked white silk shirt and a pair of tight-fitting jeans that hugged his narrow hips and long, lean thighs. What he did for jeans would have sold racks of them. Polly's stomach performed a somersault. 'Pardon?' she queried.

'The book.'

'Oh, that.' Carelessly she put it down. 'I didn't know you wore jeans.'

He shrugged rather tensely, skimming a beautifully shaped hand off a denim-clad hip. 'Since you are not strong enough yet to dress, I thought I would be more casual.'

As she began to rise he curved an arm round her and the next minute she was airborne. 'You know, I can walk—I'm not crippled!' she protested breathlessly.

'The doctor said that you were to take everything very slowly. You can't want to risk a relapse. Our climate is not kind to the delicate.' Ebony lashed blue eyes travelled reprovingly over her pink face.

There was a whirring sensation behind her temples. The sunwarmed scent of him was in her nostrils, the virile heat of his flesh penetrating the light kimono robe she wore. The whirring became a thrumming pulsebeat throughout her tautened body. She was unnaturally stiff by the time he stowed her on a tumbled pile of silk cushions in a vast and austere room.

Desire was in her like a dark enemy he had implanted, a hot, feverish intoxication of every sense that left her reeling on the lowering realisation that until she met Raschid she had been part stranger even to herself. While she lay in her bed and he remained distantly polite, denying that her vulnerability existed had been easier. But when he touched her those proud self-delusions shattered. Then, as now, her awareness of him was so pronounced that it was an exquisite pain. And worst of all, some treacherously feminine trait in her gloried unreservedly in the race of her pulses, the dryness in her mouth and the crazy acceleration of her heart. Tearing her attention from him, she squashed those renegade feelings. The power of them terrified her even as they pointed out all over again what she had not felt for Chris.

Raschid folded down lithely and food started to arrive, borne by half a dozen servants. 'Had I known in advance that you would be well enough to join me this evening, I would have located a table and chairs,' he told her.

Dear heaven, had Susan MacKenzie somehow prompted him to this invitation? Polly's cheeks flamed.

'I expect that you have noticed that these apartments are not very modern.'

'I assume Berah preferred the traditional look,' Polly said, woodenly dismissive.

Visibly he tautened. 'Berah and I lived in a different wing of the palace.' He paused. 'After her death I chose to embrace new surroundings.'

Had he set up a holy, untouchable shrine in the old? Polly had long since discounted Jezra's assertion of Raschid's unhappiness with her predecessor. Four years ago, Jezra had been a child scarcely qualified to make that judgement. His undoubted sensitivity to any reminder of Berah was more revealing. Exactly where did this female in Paris fit in? Then she was being very naïve, wasn't she? Raschid was a very male animal. His sexual needs had not diminished with his first wife's death. A mistress would have been more a necessity than an indulgence, Polly thought darkly. Fortunately she really didn't care what he did as long as he left her alone.

'In comparison with your home, perhaps you find this household rather primitive,' he continued, still only receiving half her attention. 'These things have never been important to me. My needs are few. I have never been much of a consumer of luxury goods. Then I spend little time here.'

What was suddenly freezing her into a polar absence of expression was the amazing sight of Raschid embarrassed and fighting to maintain his usual air of daunting gravity. For some reason he had started noticing that his home had all the warm welcome of Frankenstein's castle. 'Oh, I think this is very comfortable . . . cosy,' she added in a generous rush, as if they were not seated on a carpet in the middle of an echoing and three-quarters-empty room.

'I usually eat with my father.'

It was a rare titbit of personal information. Raschid never talked about himself. From Jezra Polly had learnt that he had spent the early years of his life in the desert, travelling with Nurbah's relatives, the only allowance made towards his status that of an accompanying tutor. At ten he had gone to a military academy in Saudi Arabia, concluding his education with a degree in business management. The two brothers had enjoyed incredibly different childhoods. King Reija had evidently ruled against the dangers of too great a Western influence being allowed sway over his son and heir. But Raschid's childhood impressed Polly as having been distinctly grim and cheerless, high on character-building discipline and low on parental attention and carefree pursuits. It explained that gravity beyond his years.

'You didn't have to eat with me,' she said flatly, shaking irritably free of her irrelevant thoughts. 'After all, you told me that this would be on the proscribed list. Of course, Asif always eats with Chassa when he's at home. But then, I expect he picked up bad habits, being educated in England.'

At her reference to his brother, his lean features shuttered, his mouth hardening. 'I don't deny that Asif is more Westernised, but he is not someone whom I presently wish to discuss.'

Obstinately she persisted, 'Why? Is he in some sort of trouble?'

He sent her a gleaming glance, refusing to be drawn.

'I found him very pleasant.'

A sardonic brow lifted. 'The art of being pleasant has always been at Asif's fingertips. He has infinite charm with your sex when he chooses to employ it. Now, as you know, I leave for New York tomorrow.' An odd little silence stretched like a bed of nails beneath her nerves. Her smile began to feel frozen on her lips. 'When I return perhaps you will have made alterations here. You have a free hand. I would wish you to feel at home for as long as you are here,' he concluded smoothly.

It was a speech like a scorpion with a sting in its tail. *For as long as you are here.* It reverberated through Polly. Was he making a discreet reference to a divorce in the not too distant future? What else could he be doing? Their marriage as such had not even begun, and already he was foreseeing its conclusion. A fierce and blinding wave of anger consumed her. 'Exactly how long do you expect me to feel at home?' she demanded. 'Don't please feel the need to talk in polite riddles. If you want a divorce, just say so!'

Raschid did not react to her fury. His eyes remained steady. 'I am not presently thinking of a divorce.'

'What did you raise my hopes for, then?' she slammed back, outraged by his coolness. 'I'd like a time limit to the sentence.'

'Until we tire of each other, then,' he said softly. 'These attractions fade as swiftly as the flowers that bloom in the desert after rain. What is between us will pall just as quickly. It would not be fair of me to pretend otherwise. I do not wish to hurt your feelings, Polly.'

Blindly she studied the glass of lemonade in her hand. How could he employ such brutal, demeaning candour and contrive to do so with that quality of apparent sincerity? Was she ever to understand Raschid? She was trembling with a mass of conflicting emotions. Hatred rose uppermost. Her pride revolted against the implication that she was a purely sexual being, put on this earth for his gratification, an object to be lifted and discarded at whim. He had never planned to give their marriage a fighting chance. He had never envisaged permanent ties. To tell her that openly was to offend her beyond forgiveness.

'You don't have that power,' she parried through compressed lips.

'Perhaps you will now practise the same honesty with me.' He surveyed her with unreadably bright eyes, but the tension in the air was tangible. 'About Chris.'

Her brain in a dazed whirl, Polly echoed, 'Chris?'

# CHAPTER FIVE

'You called for him when you were delirious. Had you not been ill, I would have requested this explanation sooner,' Raschid advanced harshly. 'Naturally I wish to know exactly what your relationship with this man entailed.'

The mists of incomprehension cleared. Polly's colour fluctuated wildly. Had she called for Chris? While she was ill, had her subconscious mind teemed with the conflict of her unsettled feelings? From beneath her lashes she studied the brooding cast of his features. So this was what had lain behind the constraint she had sensed, this was the subject postponed until she was on the road to recovery. His suspicions roused, he had gritted those even white teeth and simmered over the idea that his bride might not be as pure and untouched as he considered his medieval due. What he really meant was, had she slept with him? The offensively arrogant bite of his demand that she explain herself chased away her momentary embarrassment.

'Polly!'

'My relationship with Chris is nothing to do with you.' Swept by an unfamiliar sense of feminine power, she met his charged stare. 'You bought my disposable future, not my past,' she retorted drily.

In a controlled movement Raschid sprang upright. 'Are you in love with him?' he raked at her. 'I will have an answer from you. You are my wife!'

But only when it suits you to throw it at me, she thought with an inner venom that slightly shook her. In

76

love. In love with love. Was that what she had been? It was still none of Raschid's business.

'Look at me! I will not address the back of your head. But I will have an answer,' he assured her grimly. 'That is my right.'

Angrily she glanced up. 'What's it to you if I am madly in love with him?'

His eyes blazed at her, a formidable and powerful anger written into every taut line of his aggressive stance. 'And with this you expected to establish a relationship with me?' he seethed across the room at her. 'I told myself that I would not judge you unheard again, but I was foolish to doubt my own perception.'

He was like a coiled whip ready to unfurl. She was on dangerous ground. Her malicious intent to confirm his suspicions suddenly lost its strength. Since it must be obvious that Chris had not returned her feelings, wouldn't she end up looking rather pathetic? There could be no vengeful satisfaction in such a conclusion. Realising how she had cornered herself by losing her temper, she said irritably, 'For goodness' sake, I was only joking! Do we need the three-act drama?'

Suddenly alarmingly close, Raschid dropped down in front of her and repeated, 'Joking?'

Polly attempted to retreat. A ruthless hand caught in her hair and blue eyes of feral brilliance flared into her. 'Explain the joke,' he invited.

'Joke wasn't the right word,' she altered in desperation. 'You don't understand...'

His long fingers tightened their hold. 'Make me,' he suggested lethally.

'Chris and I grew up together. He's... he's really just a friend.'

His narrowed stare probed her defensiveness. 'I do not think that is quite the whole story.'

Polly's teeth gritted. 'It's chapter and verse.'

'I believe that you have been attracted to this man,' Raschid countered lazily. 'And perhaps if I had not come along...' The hand at the nape of her neck eased her backwards at the same time as he pressed her down on the cushions by lowering his own weight to keep her captive. 'But it is strange that I should still fail to see the humour of your...er...joke.'

'It wasn't supposed to be a joke!' In raw frustration she struggled to wriggle free.

'Truly diplomacy is not one of your talents.' A tigerish smile slanted his mouth. 'You were trying to make me jealous—you are very transparent, Polly. But how could I be jealous of my wife? You belong to me, you go nowhere without my permission.'

Enraged by his interpretation of her behaviour, she hissed, 'I wasn't trying to make you jealous, and I can't stand it when you say that I belong to you!'

'It is a fact—why quarrel with it?' As her eyes fled fearfully to the door, he murmured, 'The servants won't enter without my command.'

'How about if I scream?' she threatened wildly, her body stiffly refusing to yield to the hard lines of his.

He laughed huskily. 'They will either think that you are very passionate in my arms or that I am beating you. Neither eventuality will bring them rushing through that door.'

The predatory kindling of his measuring scrutiny was not lost on her. She was terrified of responding to him, terrified of a self-betrayal she would find impossible to forgive or excuse. All that Raschid deserved was a display of cool contempt and indifference. He tasted her angrily parted lips with urgent brevity.

She twisted her head away, fighting the leap of her pulses. 'No!'

His fingers framed her cheekbone. 'From the first desire was there between us. A day will come when the very last word you wish to employ with me is no,' he declared.

As he captured her mouth again, skilled and un-hurried, then ravagingly sweet and insistent, the taut stasis of her body heated to the abrasively masculine lure of his. She could not deny him. Within seconds she was lost to that violent and intense mingling of sensation and emotion which thundered through her veins like the beat of stormy seas. Her slender length in thrall to the in-credibly sensual exploration of his hands, she clung to him. His breath rasped in his throat as he released her, sinking back to narrowly observe her drugged eyes and hectically flushed cheeks.

'And truly it is not a word you use when you most need to use it.' Arrogant mastery burnishing his gaze, his mobile mouth quirked amusedly. 'Then I shouldn't begin what I can't finish. You are not yet convalesced to that degree. But how I wish it were not so!'

Polly pulled the loosened robe clumsily round her again. Her breasts were achingly full from his caresses, a hot, shivery weakness was tremulously besetting her lower limbs. The incisive imprint of him was still on her like a burning brand.

'Must you look at me as if you have been assaulted against your will?' Raschid said drily. 'At least be honest with yourself.'

Her darkened eyes embittered, she whispered, 'You'd be surprised how honest I can be with myself. I know how a whore feels now.'

After an arrested pause, he disconcerted her entirely by flinging back his imperious dark head and laughing with rich appreciation. Indignantly she leapt up—or at least she tried. He spanned her waist with firm hands that imposed restraint. 'Forgive me. It was not very kind of me to laugh at your exit line,' he conceded not quite levelly. 'But sometimes when you intend to be very rude, you are instead very funny. I was supposed to be angry? Shocked?'

'With your experience of that breed of women, I guess not!' she threw in a tempestuous rage. 'But I have no plans to join the ranks. If you had any decency at all, you'd leave me alone. Now will you get your rotten, womanising hands off me?'

An anger that knocked hers into obscurity had wiped the glimmering warmth from his eyes. It dimmed slightly, however, as she hurled the last line at him. 'It is fortunate that I have become well acquainted with your habit of speaking first and thinking second. But I warn you, some day that tongue of yours will take you too far.'

'You aren't going to keep me quiet!' Polly gasped furiously. 'You don't want a wife—you never did. We both know that divorce is on the cards. Since you've been so refreshingly frank, I'll return the compliment. I'm not playing the game, Raschid. I'm not sharing your bed because you've got nothing better to do when you're here. Our marriage is a total farce, and if you push me, I won't fit in with the charade in any way. I'm warning you as well.'

'Don't threaten me.' It was velvety soft. 'Don't ever threaten me.'

Prickles of alarm were running up and down her spine while he silently studied her. His hands slid from her. 'I must confess that I forgot my sister's foolish words to you,' he breathed in exasperation.

What had preoccupied her unceasingly in recent days was the merest triviality to him. Fiercely she stiffened and thrust up her chin. 'Please don't insult my intelligence with the lies your loving sister was happy to swallow!'

'You know me so little still?' The hauteur of his look drove colour into her strained face. 'I might have believed that you had a better knowledge of my character.'

How? He was a law unto himself, a parcel of contra-dictions. He had a mind with more twists than the Hampton Court maze, a mind which a scheming Borgia would have envied. A mind which tied Polly up in knots.

'That woman does not exist in my life,' he said coolly. 'I do not pretend to have lived as a celibate, but I would not lie with my wife and then lie with another woman. The concept of that fills me with distaste. I would not be unfaithful within marriage.'

She could not hold his dispassionate gaze. Her head lowered, her brain seething. He had the nine lives of a cat. By the time you had sprung the trap, he had already removed himself to a place of safety. He had dispensed with his mistress. King Reija had played a winning hand. You had to take your hat off to the old gentleman—he knew his son. Enter Polly, exit blonde Parisienne. Convinced that he fully intended to carry on the affair, Polly had worked herself up into a state of righteous indignation. Ignominiously routed, she now only longed for escape. 'I'm tired,' she told him.

'Stay where you are.'

'No, I really feel we've done the topic to death,' she muttered.

A dark brow lifted. 'Though it was not greatly on your mind when you were in my arms, was it?' Raschid hazarded grimly. 'Surely we may deal together better than this?'

A tide of burning moisture stung Polly's sensitive eyelids. She was all mixed up, but she refused to be ashamed of her suspicion. Raschid sought no closer ties with her. She couldn't be blamed for distrust. Not when it was so humiliatingly obvious that the only role she was to be permitted to play was that of mistress within marriage.

He released his breath. 'You do seem tired. This evening has been too great a strain for you.'

Before she could object he had swept her up in his arms. She felt like a toy about to be stowed back on the appropriate shelf in a cupboard, and forgotten. She didn't speak when he laid her down on the bed.

'I will phone you while I am away,' he told her.

'Don't bother,' she retorted from the depths of her bitter turmoil. 'No pretence—remember? And I certainly don't want the reminders.'

'As you wish.'

Even if he had slammed the door it would have made her feel better. But Raschid did not sink to childish displays. He was too disciplined, too self-contained to require the outlet. Dinner had been laden with calamity like the wedding and the wedding night. There was no meeting point between them. He wouldn't permit one. He wouldn't give an inch on the terms he had dictated at Ladybright.

With his essential detachment that supplied him with no problems. Polly was different. She couldn't cope with the knowledge that Raschid expected her to switch her emotions off and let him make love to her. She coped even worse with the awareness that she wanted him, as she had never wanted Chris. The missing ingredient in her response to Chris was all too prominent with Raschid. Sexual attraction.

As the clear call of the muezzin called the faithful to prayer at dawn, Polly was still lying hollow-eyed and wide awake, desperately attempting to calm the fevered rise and fall of her emotions and understand the angry hurt which lay behind her every response to Raschid.

'I'll lend you something.' Chassa rifled a unit with an obliging smile. 'Why didn't you tell me that you had no swimsuit? I must have a dozen.' She dropped a handful on the bed. 'I can't wait until I can wear them again.'

Glancing at Chassa's slim figure in which the evidence of her pregnancy was so slight as to be almost imperceptible, Polly smiled. 'Can't you wear them now?'

Chassa wrinkled her nose. 'I'm always very tired in the first months. It's unfortunate.' Her lustrous eyes shadowed. 'Asif is very active, he loves sports and late nights. I'm not much fun when I'm pregnant, and I shouldn't complain that he's out so often. I'm not very attractive like this.'

'That's nonsense,' Polly protested.

'You are not a man, Polly.' Chassa would not be consoled. Polly changed into the swimsuit, prudently removing her attention from Chassa's tense profile.

Asif might be technically at home, but he was rarely to be found there. In the past fortnight Polly had visited half a dozen times and Chassa had always been alone and grateful for the company. Life with the exuberant Asif was evidently not one of unblemished bliss.

With every day that filtered tranquilly by, Polly had finally conceded that what she felt for Chris was no more than the fondness of a sister for a brother, a fondness that had once been spiced with the pain of an adolescent and quite innocent crush on a childhood hero. She should have realised the difference long before now. It crossed her mind that she had been a late developer in more ways than one.

Raschid was due back at the end of the week. Polly hadn't heard a word from him. It infuriated her that, even absent, he should continue to dominate her thoughts. But what else did she have to think about? An hour learning Arabic every day? Jezra attended an exclusive college in Jumani by day and either entertained friends of her own age group or watched television by night.

'Where are the children?' asked Polly, following Chassa out through her lounge to the swimming pool in the courtyard beyond. As a rule the two toddlers were outside playing.

'With their nurse. They tired me out this morning. I should have invited you,' Chassa hesitated. 'You are very fond of children, aren't you?'

Polly laughed. 'Something of a necessity with three sisters and a baby brother, and your daughters are gorgeous little girls.'

Slipping down into the inviting depths of the pool, she heaved a blissful sigh. The cool lap of the water was wondrously soothing and after swimming back and forth for a while, she floated, grateful for the sunglasses that cut out the blinding glare of the sun reflecting on the water.

'You are a good friend,' Chassa remarked out of the blue. 'You don't ask questions even when you know that there is something wrong. I am glad of your tact.'

Polly sealed her lips on a startled comment. The compliment was unearned. She had not suspected that there was anything seriously amiss between Chassa and Asif; all couples had ups and downs. She was really far too bound up in her own anxieties to be that observant. 'If there's ever anything I can do...' she said quietly.

'You are kind, but it will work out,' Chassa assured her tightly.

What would work out? Once more Polly had that feeling that someone was assuming that she was more informed than she indeed was. It was extremely frustrating. The reflection led her back to thoughts of Berah, whom she still knew nothing about. Her curiosity was only natural, wasn't it? Why shouldn't she pump Chassa? Every time she came here she retreated from the temptation. She cleared her throat. 'Do you mind if I ask you what Berah was like?'

Chassa sat up on her lounger. 'Berah?' she repeated in surprise.

'Raschid never mentions her, and I don't like to ask,' Polly confided truthfully. 'Did you even know her very well? I realise that she died soon after you married Asif.'

'I met her only on a few occasions. When I was a teenager I spent my summers here while my parents were abroad. It was really so that Asif and I could get to know each other a little,' Chassa volunteered wryly.

'But Raschid didn't know Berah before they married, did he?'

Chassa grimaced. 'Prince Achmed is very old-fashioned. Berah was brought up very strictly. She was not educated like you or me—her father didn't approve of educating women.' She sighed. 'You ask me what she was like. She was beautiful, feminine but very quiet, not open.'

'Jezra told me that she was often very depressed.'

Chassa paled. 'Yes, that is true. She became...slightly unbalanced by her craving for a child. She loved Raschid very much—she idolised him. It was very sad,' she said uncomfortably, her gentle eyes troubled, 'but I think that many women have coped with heavier blows. Asif hated her. He said that she changed Raschid forever—I don't know. I have never known Raschid different from the man he is now...' Her sleek dark head turned almost with relief at the sound of footsteps.

Asif strolled out to the poolside, debonair in a fashionable white suit. He was swinging his sunglasses in one hand. When he saw Polly, he struck a theatrical attitude of astonishment. 'I don't believe it! It is Polly the illusion. We hear about you, we talk about you, and how often do we see you?' His grin was ebullient. 'But since your arrival you have been a rare source of entertainment. On that point I can reassure you.'

'Polly is often here. Why do you say these things?' Chassa enquired stiffly, studiously avoiding looking anywhere near her extrovert husband. 'What must she think of you?'

He laughed. 'I was joking. I don't have to treat Polly like a stuffed-shirt guest. She shouldn't need to be told that I'm delighted to find her here. But if I were you, Polly...' As he hitched his immaculate pants to hunker down, his tone became one of exaggerated confidentiality, 'I would vacate the water at speed. You may have noticed that Raschid is not the most liberated of men, and he has this marked tendency to believe that no man can look at you without being inspired by the kind of intimate thoughts which he considers strictly his department. Why else was I barred from paying my respects personally when you were ill? He even objected to me sending you flowers—but I digress...'

'Flowers?' Polly echoed sickly.

'At this very moment Raschid is probably trying to find you,' he continued, unconscious of the brick he had dropped. 'Take it from me, my pool is not where he wants to strike oil.'

Asif had sent the flowers. She could have sunk in her chagrin. Asif's droll delivery further slowed up her thinking processes. 'Raschid's back?' she ejaculated sharply. 'Early?'

She hauled herself out of the water without bothering to wade to the steps. Chassa tossed her a towelling robe. 'I'll send your clothes over later.'

Polly twisted the moisture out of her hair with a nerveless hand. Raschid was five days early and she hadn't heard the jet. How the heck could she have missed hearing it? She fled indoors in panic. He had simply taken the hint about the flowers. Her annoyance was out of all proportion to the embarrassing discovery. A cover-up for the discomfiture of learning that Berah sounded as if she had been the perfect wife aside of her surely understandable grief over her childless state? Beautiful, feminine, quiet, adoring. Polly skidded to a breathless halt inside the bedroom. Half-way out of the robe, she froze in dismay when the door opened.

Crusader-blue eyes flamed over the shapely curves almost indecently defined by the clinging swimsuit. The tightened buds of her nipples were clearly outlined for his appraisal. In a sudden defensive movement, she covered herself again.

'You have been swimming?'

'Yes.' Scorched by the sensual burn of Raschid's outright stare, Polly heard her voice emerge stiltedly. 'I didn't hear the jet landing.'

'We landed at the airport. I had business in Jumani.' His hand lifted to the gold *agal* binding his *kaffiyeh*. Removing it, he cast both aside, his whole attention relentlessly fixed on her as he crossed the room.

Silently he peeled the garment's crumpled edges out of her tight hold and parted them. Slowly he tipped the robe off her taut shoulders to let it fall. Naked desire fired his eyes. A heartbeat later she was in his arms, her stunned protest drowned by the insistent possession of his mouth. Devastated by the smouldering charge of that driving kiss, she trembled violently. He rocked her from her head to her toes with the force of his passion. Her response was intuitive, spontaneous. For a timeless space there was nothing but him, and the world had shrunk to the boundaries of that savage embrace.

Loosening the halter ties at the nape of her neck, his hands impatiently pushed the fabric down to her waist, skimming back up over her narrow ribcage to enclose the tiptilted swell of her breasts. He made a wholly masculine sound of satisfaction. His thumbs drew down over the tumescent nipples he had revealed and her knees buckled, her fingers grabbing at his shoulders for support. His lips broke from hers only as he lifted her and brought her down on the bed.

Her hands flew up to cover her breasts. The glitter of his eyes marked the gesture as he stepped back and began to undress. 'Rewarded with this enthusiasm, I may forgive much,' he breathed huskily. 'Vocal as you were on our wedding night, you would have proved a willing partner had providence not stricken you with illness.'

'That's a lie!' she spluttered, her eyes wide with trepidation.

'I will enjoy disproving the claim. I think playing the shrinking martyr threatened by her husband's lust will be a role you find difficult to maintain when you leave this room again.' Almost casually Raschid leant forward and closed a hand round the slim ankle snaking back as she attempted to escape over to the far side of the bed. In his vibrant amusement, his slashing smile was pure-bred primitive. 'But I confess I had not expected you to make this quite so entertaining.'

Impotently Polly tried to kick. The temper which only surfaced in her with him had taken over. He held her fast, black-lashed eyes of azure glinting with a humour that was more maddening to Polly than anything he had either done or said. 'How foolish of me not to guess. This is in all probability your fantasy.'

'F-fantasy?' she parroted, aghast.

'Your cruel Arab husband spreadeagling you by force upon the bed to have his wicked way with you while remaining indifferent to your pleas for mercy,' he clarified with velvet-dark satire.

Polly was for once open-mouthed and speechless.

His fingers released her ankle only as he gracefully came down on the bed to trap her squirming body in place. 'Are you not to scream at this point?' he provoked. 'Then I see your dilemma. The evil ravisher is supposed to inspire you only with revulsion. I hate to discredit your performance when you have so pronounced a talent for drama, but to date it has not been a performance that convinces.'

His taunts enraged her. Her eyes were molten emerald. Her hand flashed up and was apprehended by fingers with the grip of steel. 'No,' Raschid said succinctly as if he was teaching a very basic lesson to a rebellious child.

Tears of anger and chagrin mingled in her eyes, but anger had supremacy. If the blow had connected it would have been the first violent act of a lifetime. On the other hand, when she was still in the elemental hold of a desire to commit murder she could not be expected to feel ashamed for failing. 'You hateful brute!' she snapped.

His teeth grazed the fingertips of the hand he had imprisoned. The tip of his tongue roamed a tantalising passage down into the centre of her palm where his warm lips circled sensuously. 'We have been married almost a month. I've been very patient.'

'You haven't even asked how I feel!' Polly was shaking and yet her limbs were reed-taut. The erotic seduction of that lazy caress sparked a clenched tight excitement in the pit of her stomach.

'Lively?' he mocked. 'I do not think that your energy level is under dispute.'

'This is disgusting!' she hurled contemptuously.

Eyes a mere glimmer of dense blue gleamed. Raschid bit her forefinger in teasing punishment. 'A man might have to suspend you by the heels over a dry well to receive the truth, but fortunately for you I am infinitely more subtle.' He rolled over, capturing her to the lean, bronze muscularity of his body, one firm hand anchored into the tangle of her hair. 'I think you have spent a long time asleep, Polly, and it is I who will wake you up,' he emphasised, and the purpose marking his compellingly masculine features was no longer even superficially indulgent.

'I can't stop you, can I?' she flashed.

'But you don't want me to stop,' he gibed, his hand smoothly gliding down to divest her of the swimsuit.

He bent his head over the tender flesh he had earlier caressed. His tousled hair was midnight-black against her pale skin. Tormented by the sight, Polly shut her eyes. His tongue lashed the sensitive peaks, his fingers shaping the rounded globes with a gentleness that was her undoing. Then his lips closed there, teasing her into a mindless delirium. His mouth against her breast was an indescribable pleasure, engulfing her in instantaneous heat. Before very long her awareness encompassed only the satin texture of his skin, the rich silk of his hair and the feverish excitement which drove out all rational thought. By then her lips needed no coaxing to meet his, nor her arms any encouragement to hold him.

His hand stroked over her stomach and gently to the very heart of her. It was an intimacy beyond anything she had ever imagined. She twisted against him, instinctively arching in wanton invitation to that intimate exploration. Tiny sounds broke unwittingly from her throat. Tremors of delight surged over her, growing stronger by the second.

Spontaneously she pressed her lips to the smoothness of his shoulder. With an inarticulate little cry she drank in the scent of the sandalwood which clung evocatively to his skin. His tormenting mouth teased at her throat as she writhed out of control. Sensation heaped upon sensation in an ever-climbing spiral of desire until an agonising ache mounted an unbearable tension in her limbs. Her nails dug involuntarily, pleadingly into the corded muscles of his back.

'Give yourself to me,' he commanded hoarsely.

She raised her lips and he rewarded her obedience with a wild hunger that melted her into honeyed fluidity. He parted her thighs with his and urged her up to receive him. She responded blindly. He entered her without hesitation, and the pain of that alien intrusion partly diminished the frenzy of need that ruled her. But he carried her remorselessly through that barrier, checking her cry of denial with the brand of his mouth. Under the rhythmic stroke of his possession she reached that higher plane she had strained towards in an explosion of ecstasy and fell into that intense, drowning pleasure as if she had been waiting for that moment all her life. Raschid attained that same plateau in silence, only the rough rasp of his breathing and the heavy thud of his heart against her breast betraying him.

He studied her slumbrously, both gravity and a glint of light-hearted indulgence mingling in his shamelessly steady scrutiny. Then he pressed a kiss to her damp temples. 'You please me,' he murmured quietly.

Hard on the heels of dizzy satisfaction came the jolting return to sentience. Those three little words which he lazily bestowed acted on Polly like a clarion call. In that first smarting encounter with self-loathing, she pulled away, only to be deprived of the point by Raschid's abrupt move to accomplish the same feat.

As he left the bed, she clawed the sheet over her nakedness. He was a pagan golden outline in the late afternoon shadows. She pushed her hot face into a cool pillow and the world was still whirling round her. Incredulity and embarrassment held her. He had accurately forecast her surrender, her—why didn't she face it?—her enjoyment. Her own weakness seemed to tower above her in a monolith of shame. Dear heaven, she had lost all control. She had held nothing back.

The mattress gave beside her. 'Polly... my bed is not a burrow and you are not a small furry creature. Sit up.'

She noticed the way in which her bed had suddenly become his bed. Turning reluctantly back, she was bedazzled by the breathtaking river of diamonds and emeralds sparkling white and green fire against his tanned hand. Dumbfounded, she stared.

'I chose it for you in New York.' The metallic coldness of the exquisite necklace chilled her skin, his fingertips light beneath her hair as he fastened the clasp.

A phone call would have been cheaper. Clearing her clogged vocal cords, she whispered, 'It's fantastic!'

'There are earrings and a bracelet to match,' he said offhandedly.

Rewarded for her capitulation as a favoured concubine might have been a century earlier, Polly was nauseated. Her eyes gritted up. Suspicion loomed large. What had Raschid got up to in New York? If she had dared she would have slung it back and suggested that he keep the sparklers for his next mistress.

She wound herself in the sheet, trailing it off the bed, and escaped into the bathroom. In the mirror she looked the same, and yet she would never be the same again. Her fingers rested on the jewels shining with blinding brilliance and shakily she took the necklace off. Desire had stolen her wits. But she had wanted him—oh, how she had wanted him! Angry, bitter, frightened or unhappy, it made no difference. Still she wanted him. What had he done to her? What craziness came over her when he touched her? Buried in the welter of her frantic thoughts, she stepped beneath the cooling gush of the shower. A minute later strong arms encircled her from behind.

'Raschid?' she yelped.

'I can safely promise you that you will not share a shower with anyone else.'

'I don't want to share one with you either!' she blazed back in sudden fury. 'Are you telling me that there's a water shortage?'

'Polly,' he implored unsteadily, 'don't make me laugh.'

He kissed her breathless. Her centre of gravity went spinning off into infinity and her hands laced into his wet hair. Later she didn't remember leaving the shower. Raschid tumbled her down and took her wildly on the soft, deep carpet. She clung to him in a storm of passion, every inhibition banished by more and more and even more of that mindless, self-seeking pleasure. In the aftermath the recessed downlighters on the ceiling above shone down on her like so many accusing eyes. Proprietorial fingers were roaming over her sweat-slicked skin with a tenderness at variance with the sensual savagery he had introduced her to.

It was a dream she wanted censored, a dream she wanted to wake up from to discover that she was not, after all, this woman. But she was—she was this woman, defenceless in a man's grasp, bewitched by a magnetic sexual spell into betraying every principle she had ever believed in.

# CHAPTER SIX

'SMILE!' A blunt fingertip playfully scored the tremulous curve of her lower lip.

Snaking free, Polly snatched up a fleecy towel. 'I have to endure everything else, but I don't have to smile!'

Raschid tugged her back with an indolently powerful hand. 'Repeat that.'

Her teeth set together in thwarted frustration.

'Yes, you suffer with such masochistic fervour,' he murmured silkily. 'I cannot wonder at your sudden silence.'

Released, she stalked back into the bedroom to straighten the bed. Listening to the beat of the shower on the tiles, she slid back beneath the sheet. The very bedding bore his scent—evocative, intimate, inescapable. Like an addict Polly breathed it in until she realised what she was doing, and then she wanted to cry. Thinking about Berah, who had reputedly wept the Volga dry, she quickly stifled the feeble urge.

Some time later Raschid inched back the sheet and flipped her over with cool hands. He extracted a lingering kiss before she could rescue her breath to object. 'I can't stay,' he admitted. 'I have a report to give to my father. I'm dining with him. I will try not to be late.'

'Take all night,' she suggested thinly. 'I'm amazed that I was sandwiched into your busy itinerary.'

He laughed softly, his brilliant eyes untamed in their vitality. 'For some things, there is always time.'

Impervious to her mutinous fury, he considerately covered her up again. Angrily she sat up, anchoring the sheet beneath her arms. 'I think I'm entitled to a room of my own. There's a dozen available.'

'But then I would be put to the inconvenience of fetching you.' Calmly he finished dressing, attaching a curved dagger, an ornate silver *khanjar*, to his belt. Straightening, he flipped the edges of his flowing gold-bordered black cloak back over his shoulders. The snap and crackle in the atmosphere appeared to leave him untouched.

'I hate you for this!' Abruptly Polly let loose her pent-up rage and frustration. 'I've never hated anyone in my life, but I hate you!' Her attack throbbed with feeling.

'A category all to myself? I am honoured, and I do understand. It was very selfish of me not to consider your feelings and make it a brutal rape.' Raschid flashed her a glittering glance of sheer masculine provocation and taking advantage of her thunderstruck silence, he pointed out equably, 'You'll be safe in the shower now,' before he departed.

The minute he walked out of the door Polly believed he forgot her existence, just as he had contrived to forget it for the past two weeks. He treated her like a partner in a casual affair. She didn't feel like a wife. How could she? He didn't behave like a husband. But he had warned her how it would be in advance. He had warned her that love and sentiment would play no part in their alliance. And she had accepted those terms—mutely, unthinkingly, her head buried in the sand.

The instant he left the room, the stimulus of anger mysteriously ebbed away. Behind it lurked a great well of unbearable loneliness. She had made a devil's bargain. It was costing her more than her freedom. It was stealing away all peace of mind, all pride. She needed those pretences he had disdained. What she could not stand was that he should contentedly remain utterly detached from her. It was the ultimate rejection.

It was late when he returned. Polly didn't hear him enter the lounge. He moved like a night-prowling cat. Looking up, she saw him, darkly stilled just inside the pool of light shed by the lamp to one side of her. Her pulses quickened, her breath catching in her mouth. She told herself it was fright.

'Some unexpected guests arrived,' he imparted. 'It would have been impolite for me to leave sooner.'

Polly gave a shrug. Her earlier emotionalism had hardened into a cold and bitter implacability. 'You don't need to explain yourself to me.'

His eyes narrowed. 'I consider it simple courtesy to do so.'

It was Polly who went pink. She gathered up the letter she had been writing, intending to remove herself. Raschid moved a staying hand and sank down on the seat opposite. 'I was most disturbed to learn that you did not leave the palace during my absence. You had only to order a car.'

'Until recently I didn't feel up to much.'

'Surely you might have enjoyed a drive? You are not living in the Bastille,' he said drily. 'It isn't good for you to be shut up after your illness.'

Polly leapt with grim satisfaction into reply. 'Nobody told me that I could order a car, and where would I have gone? Jumani?' she enquired. 'I don't have any money.'

Faint colour barred his cheekbones. 'I should have thought of these things. You have reason to complain.'

'I wasn't complaining, I was merely stating facts.'

'I should have phoned you. You could have reminded me.' He sighed. 'As a rule I am not lacking in manners.'

Incensed by the information that he regarded a couple of phone calls to his wife as a duty courtesy, Polly stiffened. 'It's all right, I didn't really notice.'

Unanticipated humour lightened his features. 'I feel duly punished now, Polly. For a deliberate omission not to be noticed is a just reward.'

The force of that unchoreographed charisma of his nearly splintered through her cold front. She wanted to smile back. The acknowledgement unnerved her. His attraction was a hundred times more powerful because he seemed quite unaware of it. She could not help comparing him with Asif, whose charm was boyishly calculated and gilded by unhidden conceit. Raschid's sophistication was not Asif's. Raschid might be cultured and cynical, but he would never possess his brother's studied air of bored languor. His vibrancy, shielded by that cool austerity, beckoned to Polly with the burning heat of a fire on a winter's day.

'Tomorrow I will take you into Jumani. There are furniture warehouses there.' He surveyed the shadowy room and the cosy corner Polly had incongruously set up for her comfort with grim disfavour. 'I have never entertained here. I have never even used this room before.'

It was so wretchedly typical of Raschid to reappear the very epitome of well-bred and reasonable behaviour. Gone was the passionate lover, who had taken her by storm and ruthlessly rejoiced in conquest. An odd little shiver, indecently reminiscent of anticipation in reverse, assailed her. Hurriedly she got up. 'Fine. I'm going to bed now, unless you have some objections.'

He eyed her set face unreadably. 'Go to bed if you wish. I have work to do.'

From the door she glanced back. He was motionless by the window, a solitary dark figure in splendid isolation. He didn't need her, he didn't need anybody. But still that view of him unawares tugged wilfully at her heartstrings. She couldn't sleep. It was one in the morning and he was working. Even if he had slept during the flight, time zones played havoc with anybody's system. Polly curled up in a damp heap round a pillow.

Furniture, she reflected incredulously. He talked about her refurnishing when a divide the width of the universe stretched between them. Did he think that all he had to do to keep her in contented subjection was throw a king's ransom in jewellery at her and let her spend a fortune on a home which was not her home and never would be? Did he think that that would miraculously convert her to her lot? Could he really believe that she valued herself so low?

Around dawn she discovered that she was wrapped round Raschid instead of the pillow. There was not a lot of excuse for that in a bed six feet wide. As she began gingerly to detach herself, he turned over and anchored her to his lithe, brown body, murmuring something indistinct in Arabic and then her name. He kissed her, and her toes curled shamelessly. While she was trying to uncurl them, he darted his tongue hungrily into the moist recesses of her mouth and what her toes were doing receded in immediate importance for a very long time.

He sauntered fully dressed to the foot of the bed. Polly's heartbeat tipped against her breastbone. 'What time is it?' she whispered.

'Almost half-past six.'

'Is that all?' Gratefully her eyelids dropped again.

'It's the coolest part of the day. Later it will be too hot for you. I always go riding in the morning. You can join me. That is not a pleasure you have to do without here. Have you inspected the stables yet?'

She didn't want to look at him. As memories touched wilfully and cruelly on her all she wanted to do was curl up and die, preferably without an audience. 'I'm not a very good rider.'

'That's not important.' But he couldn't keep the surprise from his voice.

'Apart from that, I'm not in the mood to go riding,' she muttered. 'Enjoy yourself.'

'You are not making this any easier for either of us,' he breathed. 'You are being childish.'

'It's funny how I'm always being childish when I disagree with you or obtrude as an individual,' Polly said bitterly from the depths of the bed.

Her tiredness put to flight, she tossed for a while before getting up. She was being foolish. She was driving a further wedge between them. Twenty minutes later she arrived breathlessly in the domed porch, just in time to see Raschid swinging himself up into the saddle of a magnificent black thoroughbred. The stallion's sleek lines were pure Arabian, beauty and stamina superbly matched. Feeling she was too late and fearful of a cool welcome, for in all likelihood the invitation had been spurred by politeness alone, Polly didn't advertise her presence.

'How very wifely!'

Startled, she spun. Asif grinned at her. 'Marzouk and Raschid are very impressive. Aren't you joining him?'

She flushed. 'No.'

'He prefers to ride alone.' Then he groaned. 'But now that you are here, naturally that will change.'

'I'm not much of a rider. I don't think I'd hamper him with my company.' She forced a smile, glad she hadn't rushed outside to publish her change of heart.

He swept a cavalier's bow with an imaginary hat. 'I wouldn't be hampered.' His brown eyes roamed appreciatively over her beautiful, laughing face and he sighed. 'You're right—I'm a hopeless flirt. I can't help it. You are much too distracting, Polly. But there are times when distractions are welcome.' He stared moodily out at Raschid cantering through the gates. 'He is a very tough act to follow.'

'Are you in competition?'

He didn't look at her. 'When Raschid was a boy, he trained his own falcon. For three months it went everywhere with him until it was tamed. He didn't mind getting clawed in the process. Our father was very proud of him. In his eyes that's the sort of behaviour that separates the men from the boys. I've still to make the grade, and the most hellish side of it is that you can't dislike Raschid for it.' He turned back to her with a rueful smile. 'For his family, even his unworthy brother, there is no sacrifice he would not make.' He evaded her gaze and sounded a rather strained laugh. 'But when the competition gets too much I can always think of the jeans.'

'The what?'

He pulled open the door, slim and elegant in his tailored riding gear. 'It is what you call an "in" joke, Polly,' he divulged, having recovered his natural buoyancy.

Unable to see anything humorous in Raschid choosing to relax in less formal clothing, Polly soon cast the trivial remark from her mind. Asif's undeniable uneasiness with her for several uncomfortable seconds had concerned her more. Was he afraid that Chassa had made indiscreet confidences? He should know his wife better. Chassa was too loyal to spill the secrets of their marriage.

Returning upstairs, she wandered into Raschid's study. It was really a library, shelved from floor to ceiling with books in several languages. She ran a thoughtful fingertip along the spines of a collection of poetry books. Berah's? Frowning, she passed on, surveying the dull appointments of the cheerless room. Apart from the telephones and the computer it was as early medieval as the rest of the place. Only the bathrooms and the kitchen quarters had been modernised—quite the opposite of Asif and Chassa's wing, which was full of designer furniture and pale, pearlised carpets. Then it was a challenge to picture Raschid against a similar backdrop.

Her hand trailed idly over the back of the chair by the desk. Did he ever think about the woman inside her pleasing shell? Her pride, her emotions, her needs? How were they to live together? How did you begin when the end was already within view? But she had begun. Why did she continue to deny the obvious? She was drowning in a physical infatuation that was terrifyingly intense. Of course she didn't know herself any more. Raschid walked into a room and there wasn't a skin cell in her body which didn't leap to that awareness. She had fought him less than she had fought herself.

Feed a cold, starve a fever; the old saying sang in her head. Could she equate a fever with an obsession? Raschid was fast becoming one. He might infuriate her, he might confound her understanding and he might sting her pride, but at no stage did he do less than fascinate her. She was on the edge of a precipice and the ground was suddenly crumbling from beneath her feet. She didn't want to be starved of him. She was already wondering how long they would have together before his next trip abroad. And if she fell in love with him, what then? Irritably she quelled that foolish worry. The more she looked back at the amount of time she had wasted mooning about over Chris, the more her stomach curdled. Her intelligence was now in firm control of her imagination and her emotions. She was not, she told herself thankfully, likely to be vulnerable in the same direction again.

'You would like tea, *lellah*?'

Zenobia smiled at her from the doorway. Reddening, Polly set down the gold pen she had absently lifted, studying it, questioning how it had got into her hand. 'Yes, that would be nice,' she said vaguely.

She kept her nose in a newspaper over breakfast. Raschid fingered through his mail and watched her in exasperation. After they had eaten, an air-conditioned limousine ferried them away from the palace at speed. They travelled along a wide thoroughfare banked by young trees being industriously watered. Taking in the size of an impressive building near completion, Polly asked what it was.

'A second hospital. It is due to open in a few weeks.'

'I'd love to see it.' Her mouth compressed. 'But I suppose that would be out of order. It wouldn't do for anybody to hint that you had a wife animated by intelligence.'

'I am not sure that it is intelligence that is animating you at this moment. I will see what I can arrange.'

As they topped the brow on a rolling hill, Jumani spread out before them. The glass of tall office blocks reflected the cloud formations. As they drove through the city her bad humour melted away as her attention roamed in eager darts. Modern skyscrapers vied with wedding-cake mosques and graceful minarets. Green expanses of parkland gleamed at intervals between the buildings. The pavements were busy and the inviting window displays she glimpsed as they sped past belonged to retail outlets that were many and varied.

'How does civilisation look now that you have got over the wall?' Raschid enquired silkily.

'It's lovely. Is that a shopping centre?' she exclaimed.

His eyes gleamed. 'Yes, Polly. Jumani has several.'

It happened slowly. He began to smile, and it was like no smile he had ever given her before. Like the sun after the rain, it was brilliant and warm.

A herd of dinosaurs could have been running amok in the city traffic—Polly would not have noticed. That smile that was neither cynical nor merely polite passed through her with the paralysing force of an electric current.

The day was an entertaining whirl. She enjoyed the tour of the warehouses and the excessive attention they received. She found herself laughing a lot, relaxing as she had never relaxed before in Raschid's company. They had lunch in a private room in a luxury hotel in the city centre; men didn't take their wives into public dining-rooms in Dharein. Raschid was not entirely at ease during the meal while the manager and waiters swarmed about them. Polly suspected he was breaking new ground. And deep in her tangled thoughts she was vaguely conscious that she would do almost anything to waken that charismatic smile again.

That evening they had barely finished dinner when Raschid's secretary, Medir, made an apologetic intrusion to mention an important phone call. Restive on her own and pleasantly relaxed, Polly decided to go for a walk in the palace gardens. In the shelter of the steep walls pepper and tamarind trees shaded fragrant oleanders with heavy pink blooms that scented the night stillness. Strolling back, she was in a brown study, and she gasped in dismay when a dark shadow moved into her path.

'Good heavens!' Clasping a helpless hand to her palpitating heart, she stared accusingly up at Raschid. 'Could you make a little more noise? You scared me— I thought I was alone out here.'

His mouth slanted. 'You are far from alone. Seif and Raoul have not been more than a few steps from you since you came outside.'

Dazedly she followed the direction of his hand and registered two more shadows over by the wall. Raschid's bodyguards.

'I am sorry if I startled you, but then you are not very observant.' His manner was teasing.

'What were they doing following me?'

'They are there for your protection.'

Before she could drily enquire if walls half-way to heaven were not protection enough, the unmistakable sound of voices raised in argument filtered down from the balcony above them. Polly recognised Asif's voice immediately.

'I believe we should go back inside,' Raschid drawled.

'All couples argue,' she said uncomfortably.

'Few as much as they do.' It was grim.

Polly frowned. 'Well, I hope you're not blaming her. She's very easygoing.'

'You don't understand the situation.'

'Educate me, then.' A silence that was deeply mortifying stretched in answer to her request.

'Don't get involved,' Raschid murmured finally. 'I voice that warning kindly.'

She felt snubbed, firmly slapped down for daring to imply that she might be sufficiently accepted as part of the family to be trusted with a confidence. In the darkness her cheeks burned. She liked Asif and Chassa, but she was neither the interfering type, nor in this case was her curiosity of the morbid variety. Picking up Raschid's tension, she had impulsively tried to share whatever was worrying him.

'Chassa does not enjoy the best of health when she is pregnant. No doubt tempers become short,' he continued smoothly.

He was only covering up; there was more to it than that. Assuming that Asif was equally keen to have a large family, surely he was guilty of selfish neglect? As Raschid curved an arm round her to guide her back indoors, Polly went suddenly still in the charged hold of an explosive acknowledgement which demolished her composure.

Where on earth would she be if she became pregnant? Already that was a possibility. She was astonished that not a single word had ever been spoken on that subject. Was Raschid under the impression that she had taken some step to avoid the danger?

'What is wrong?' He glanced down at her narrowly.

'I've just thought of something you haven't thought of.' An anger she didn't quite comprehend raced up hot and swift inside her. 'Although I must admit that on every other count you were ahead of yourself—with one strange exception. What happens to our strictly timed marriage of convenience and extreme practicality if I become pregnant?' she demanded shakily. 'Or is there a wheel within a wheel there as well? Some nefarious

plan, perhaps, to gain an heir without the encumbrance
of a wife? I imagine that would suit you very nicely.'

In the unkind clarity of the overhead light Raschid's
pallor was pronounced. His burnished eyes blazed
dangerously bright, but his response when it came was
very quiet. 'That would not be within my power, Polly.
I can give no woman a child. You stand in no danger
of becoming a mother while you live with me.'

Shock sent a wave of giddiness over her. Her fingers
tightened painfully on the stair rail. In that instant
Raschid had turned her over and inside out. She had
not been prepared; she had never even suspected. The
shock stupefied her into silence.

'I am sorry —I have embarrassed you.' His proud bone-
structure was etched hawklike beneath his golden skin,
black lashes half obscuring silvered eyes that even now
possessed a cruel capacity to interpret her every fleeting
expression. 'The manner of telling was unforgivable.
Unfortunately you took me by surprise.'

Afterwards she didn't recall climbing those stairs. In
stricken confusion she blamed herself for blundering
clumsily in where angels feared to tread. Having noted
the unusual aspect of Raschid overlooking any eventuality, might she not have made that last step in de-
duction for herself? Or would she have? Berah had been
firmly fixed in her mind as the partner unable to have
children. Only now did she see that she had had no evidence on which to base that assumption. Secure in her
misapprehension, she had repeatedly missed the point
of all that she had learnt about his first marriage.

He stood straight and still by one of the tall lounge
windows and met her uneasy gaze unflinchingly. 'You
must wonder that I should have concealed this fact at
our first meeting. Had the marriage been of my seeking
and had I viewed the tie as one of permanency, I would
naturally have told you. Then I did not consider it a
necessary explanation. But for some time I have wished

to raise the matter with you. Before I went to New York,' he quoted unemotionally. 'But you took yourself off to bed early, and I must confess that when I returned yesterday, it was my belief that you must already be aware of the fact.'

Polly was being overtaken by a hideous premonition of what his life must have been like with a wife desperate to have a baby. 'I wasn't,' she told him.

'That was obvious. Perhaps you thought that the fault lay with Berah. No, the failing was mine, not hers,' he asserted. 'But I am not, after so many years, over-sensitive to this fact now. *Insh'allah.*'

His dark-timbred drawl was the merest shade unsteady. All the over-sensitivity that ferocious pride of his denied was written in his jewelled eyes. Could she have turned time back and remained in ignorance, Polly would have done so. A floodtide of guilty tenderness pierced her deep. In its wake a nameless emotion as fierce as the desert heat clawed pain into her. But she could not reward his hard self-discipline with an emotional response. With that thought she lifted her head and said quite naturally and without a hint of sympathy, 'It's not really something that concerns us.' She paused before continuing, as continue she must, for that terrible curiosity would not leave her alone, 'But I would appreciate knowing a little more about Berah. Of course, if you don't want to talk about her, I'll understand and respect that.'

A muscle jerked tight at the corner of his mouth. 'There isn't much to tell. For an Arab woman, children are an integral part of marriage. She will measure her own importance in terms of the sons she gives her husband. Berah could not adapt to childlessness. It was not to be expected that she could do otherwise. Her sole interests revolved round home and family. Unable to have what she most desired, she was naturally unhappy.'

'When did you find out?'

'We had been married for two years. Berah had seen several different doctors, and then I . . . she did not want to tell me when the discovery was made. It was a heavy disappointment,' he confessed curtly. 'A marriage can have no meaning without children.'

'These days couples actually decide not to have children,' Polly protested lamely.

Raschid dealt her an inscrutable glance. 'Not in an Arab society, and there is a difference, is there not, in a freely made decision? In a man such a failing . . .'

'Will you stop that? Fault— failing. Will you stop talking as if it was something you could have helped?' The involuntary censure sprang from her—she could not retain it.

'I am sorry that my terminology should offend.'

'Oh, I didn't mean that, for goodness' sake!' Very close to tears, she stumbled to a halt. She hated herself for forcing Raschid to answer her questions. For a charged minute, she even hated him for confessing a very private and personal sorrow in the heroic and stoic tradition of a sinner awaiting the casting of the first stone. But above all her conflict dominated a near-overwhelming need to be physically close to him. Denied that, she could only sit there in miserable silence.

'My brother had to become a husband long before he wished for the responsibility. Chassa and Asif have paid high costs of their own. Asif was a very poor candidate for an early marriage, but stability only comes with future generations . . .' A knock sounded on the door and Medir appeared on command, wringing his hands in his usual deprecating fashion. 'Excuse me,' said Raschid, and swept out, at last releasing her from that terrible rigidity of expression and bearing. Her shoulders slumped and slowly she breathed again.

He reached for her in the night when she was pursuing sleep without success. Finally he offered her the physical contact she had craved. Of their own volition her hands

linked round the strong column of his throat, her fingertips delving into the feathery strands of his hair. Tonight, inexplicably, she was wild for him. The driving
spur of a hunger she could never have expressed in words
pulsed in her veins. Like the sea tide that beats eternally
on the shore, it was powerful, irrefutable and tenacious.
The same elemental force seemed to energise that stormy
fusion. Afterwards Raschid kept his arms wrapped
tightly round her. 'I wasn't gentle,' he breathed. 'Did I
hurt you?'

As she uttered a shy negative, the tension in him gave.
A deep and abiding sense of peace cradled her. She
buried her face in his shoulder, loving the scent and the
touch and the feel of him, but sleep was far from her.
Unbidden rose an image of a little boy with black hair
and bright blue eyes, and she crushed it guiltily in her
imagination. Raschid had lived ten years with the
knowledge of that impossibility. But wasn't it strange
that the wife who had reputedly loved him so deeply
should have selfishly wallowed in her own disappointment without caring about the damage she was inflicting on him? What kind of love was it that had
ensured that Raschid remained as painfully sensitive now
as he must have been then? Anger stirred in her and that
pain she could not comprehend kept her awake.

Conversation over breakfast was practically non-
existent. Stealing a glance at the distant cast of his hard
profile, she found it extraordinarily difficult to equate
him with the passionate lover of the night hours. All
that was light-hearted, warm and volatile in Raschid was
strictly confined to the bedroom. Beyond that door he
was courteous and aloof. Last night she had almost flung
herself at him. Now she cringed from the memory.
Perhaps it was imagination, but Raschid seemed a
thousand miles further away from her this morning.

Uncertainly she cleared her throat, and he looked up.
She couldn't quite meet his eyes. On the other hand, she

would not surrender to her own discomfiture in front of him. 'What are we doing today?' she asked brightly.

'I'm afraid I have work to attend to. You must make your own amusement.' He got up.

The silence crushed her like a giant stone. Her head bowed. She was humiliated by the assumption she had made and the chill of the snub she had invited.

He paused at the door. 'Why don't you ask Chassa to go somewhere with you? She would enjoy the diversion.'

'When I require your advice on how to get through the day, I'll ask for it,' she whispered.

Emptiness yawned inside her. When had she forgotten the rules? Their marriage was a temporary expedient. Was Raschid worried that she was in danger of forgetting the fact? He had a depth of percipience she had found uncannily acute on more than one occasion. He was highly attuned to fluctuations in behaviour and atmosphere. He watched, he waited and he deduced. An unwary word or gesture rarely escaped him.

Had it not been for what he regarded as a fatal flaw he would have dutifully remarried long ago. He would have selected someone suitable, of course. Some little twittery, submissive creature who knew her place. He wouldn't have chosen Polly. The more she thought along those lines, the more humiliated she felt. He was tearing her self-respect to ribbons. She despised herself for responding trustingly to yesterday's misleading warmth. She despised herself more for craving a smile—a stupid, worthless smile from a selfish brute who endowed her with invisibility the minute dawn broke.

In the afternoon new furniture was delivered. Polly was noisily shifting it about the lounge when he came towards her. Her heartbeat went haywire and she hated him for it.

'Why aren't the servants doing that?'

She straightened with an arctic smile. 'Because I'm enjoying doing it myself. Sorry, did the racket disturb your concentration?'

'As it happens, no. I wanted to speak to you.'

Polly lifted a footstool. 'Carry on.'

His eyes flashed. 'Put that down.'

With exaggerated care, she obeyed. Rapier-taut, he breathed. 'I owe you an apology for this morning. I am sorry if I distressed you.'

'Do I look distressed?' she demanded acidly, and turned away to plonk herself down on a seat. Once again he had disconcerted her. She could feel the tears gathering.

'I do not know how I ever thought that you were quiet,' he told her.

'The fox condemns the trap, not himself.'

'William Blake,' he identified softly. 'How sweet I roamed from...' As Polly studied him in astonishment, he shrugged. 'Poetry is much loved by my race.'

She bent her head.

'I wasn't considerate this morning,' Raschid went on.

'And of course we must stick to the letter of the law, mustn't we?' she muttered bitterly.

'No,' he contradicted. 'We have to live together, and this situation demands adjustment on both sides.'

So they had a situation now, not a marriage. She couldn't breathe, and she sniffed. With a sigh he knelt down in front of her and gently rescued the cushion she was crushing between her hands. 'You are upset. I shouldn't have married someone...'

'I'm not upset! I just don't like anybody looking at me when I'm crying!'

A shadow of that rare smile skimmed his mouth. 'Am I to leave while you compose yourself?'

'Don't be silly.' Irritably Polly wiped at her damp eyes. 'But I really don't want to hear one more time about how you didn't want to marry me. How you can say that and then...' She faltered to a blushing halt.

'Make love to you?' he interposed. 'You are very innocent, Polly.'

'No, I'm not. I'm getting educated all the time.'

Raschid sighed, 'I am a man like any other...'

'Don't worry, you're not on a pedestal!' she snapped tearfully.

His eyes glittered in driven frustration. 'You are my wife, my very beautiful wife, and it is my right...'

'To demean me by using me?' Polly inserted jerkily.

He pressed a finger to her quivering lower lip. 'That is crude, and what I have to say to you now is not easy, but I don't want you to be hurt.' He slid upright again and moved a nebulous hand. 'You must not begin imagining that you have become——' unusually, he hesitated, 'attached to me.'

Fixed by that remorseless azure gaze, she was a butterfly on the end of a twisting pin. 'I really don't think I want to hear any more of this.'

'It would only make you unhappy and it would only make me uncomfortable. I couldn't respond to those feelings. I don't have them to give. There, it is said, and you can be offended with me if you wish,' he completed harshly.

Rage had glued her tongue to the roof of her mouth. 'Attached to you?' she retorted, wondering if the parasitic choice of term was accidental or subconsciously deliberate. 'To what aspect of your truly entrancing nature could I become attached? I'm in no danger of...'

'If it is true I am glad of it, but it is not unusual for a woman to become confused about her feelings for her first lover.' As Raschid cut her off in throbbing midspeech his narrowed eyes gleamed over her fiercely.

Polly had leapt up in her fury. 'Oh, don't give me an open-ended invitation like that to ventilate my exact feelings, Raschid. It might prove seriously damaging to your ego!'

'Sexual pleasure is not restricted to those in love, Polly,' he bit out.

'All the way to Dharein with its strict moral code to find a husband preaching promiscuity!' she derided.

Dark colour had sprung up over his cheekbones. 'It was my intent to say that within a marriage where there is respect and understanding there is no shame in enjoying physical intimacy,' he returned icily.

Her chin went up, although she was shaking. 'I was taught that emotions were the distinction that lifted us up out of the animal kingdom. I'm surprised that you're not suggesting that I take a lover so that I can field-test your convictions for myself!'

Eyes an incredulous blaze of shimmering blue clashed with hers. 'The penalty for adultery in Dharein is still death.' It was a primal and savage snarl to match an anger strong enough to drain the outraged colour from her cheeks. 'But were I ever to have cause to suspect your fidelity that penalty would seem a happy exit from this life.'

The violent aggression she had incited arrested her vocal cords and her heartbeat. He released his breath in a hiss and stared at her. 'It seems that I have yet to learn appreciation of your jokes,' he enunciated through clenched teeth, the menacing cast of his hard features easing only slowly. 'But that was a provocation which would rouse any man to anger.'

Her knees were disgracefully wobbly. 'Excuse me,' she mumbled, and fled before her queasy stomach could disgrace her.

Fortunately a few gulps of fresh air out on the balcony beyond their bedroom settled her back to normality. When a hand touched her shoulder, however, she nearly leapt in the air in fright.

A firm hand steadied her. 'I believe you should abandon this tendency to refer to other men as if you are still free to think of them.'

His eyes still had a banked-down glitter. Backed up against the balcony wall, Polly was absently relieved to have a wholly clean conscience in that direction. 'Was it true what you said?' she asked.

He shifted one of his exquisitely expressive hands. 'Divorce is easy for both sexes in our society. The rights of women and children are well protected by the law. They were enshrined there centuries ago. There is little excuse for those...'

'But it does happen?'

'It has been some years since such a case has been presented, but the law still stands.'

'Well, I think...'

'I would point out that while our penal code is harsh, infringements are fewer than those in more liberal countries. Nor do our women walk in fear of sexual assault. Polly, let us discuss something on which we are less likely to argue. I don't want to argue with you.' Staring down at her vibrantly beautiful and intransigent face, he gently pushed a straying strand of hair back from her cheekbone, employing the familiarity that was almost second nature to him now.

She spun bitterly and violently away from that confident hand. 'I'd like to be on my own. I'm sure you have work to do.'

His jawline clenched. 'I came to ask you if you would like a tour of that hospital. I have arranged it.'

An anguished bitterness consumed her. Was this one of those adjustments he had mentioned? The necessity of sacrificing the occasional hour to her entertainment outside the bedroom door? Of humouring her with the pretence that he respected her as an intelligent, thinking human being? She saw herself yesterday, utterly riveted by the spellbinding charge of his full attention. She saw herself last night, slavishly eager in his arms. And she recoiled from both degrading images. This was a fever which required starvation at every possible opportunity.

Raschid had spelt out brutal facts. She ought to thank him for the short sharp shock treatment. If this agony of pain she was enduring, if this dreadful urge to claw, scratch and bite she was experiencing was the death throes of some embryonic love, she wanted no part of it, and she would have no part of such colourful fancies. There and then she made that pact with herself. The stubborn determination which was the backbone of her character underlined the decision.

In her conviction that she loved Chris, she had wished unhappiness on herself. Raschid was just as unobtainable. Did she have a masochistic streak that rejoiced in suffering? Well, if she had, on this occasion it was not about to find even a tiny outlet.

'I don't really think that that would be my style.' She produced a bright smile. 'But I hope that won't cause offence.'

'And I hope that you know what you're doing,' he intoned coldly.

# CHAPTER SEVEN

THE limousine sped through the palace gates and shot to a halt in the courtyard. Polly took a deep breath before she climbed out. Zenobia came hurrying anxiously to greet her as if she had been lying in wait.

'It is late, *lellah*,' she said breathlessly. 'You have been out for so long, and Prince Raschid returned soon after you left.'

Since Polly had planned that nifty timing she had the grace to blush. Zenobia moved to take the single package which was all her mistress had to show for an entire morning in Jumani. For three weeks a silent war of attrition had been raging between Polly and Raschid. His five-day absence at a meeting of OPEC in Geneva had proved a much-needed breathing space for her fast fraying nerves. But now he was back.

If she could, she avoided him. If she couldn't, she took refuge in a cool, offhand manner. Neither practice pleased. To a feudal male who took for granted that he should be the very centre of his wife's universe anything less was an insult. At the heart of his detachment would always dwell that chauvinistic ambivalence. But Polly had no plans to play the doormat. After all, wasn't she just riding out her time here in Dharein? Hadn't he been the one to lay down the rules? If he was now discovering that philosophy and action had little in common, the problem was his, not hers.

'I think,' Zenobia's dusky face was strained, 'Prince Raschid was concerned that you were away, *lellah*. So unfortunate,' she muttered.

Polly's eyes gleamed. Raschid wouldn't show her that he hadn't been pleased. He would be as aloof and unfailingly polite as he had been before he left. Why not? Her paltry sense of satisfaction was short-lived. For every dismissive word, every deliberate avoidance, she had paid a thousandfold when the sun went down. He punished her for her defiance with exquisite finesse and ruthless expertise during the hours of darkness.

Heat suffused her unhappy face. As long as her heart hammered crazily to the intoxication of his kisses, she had nothing to congratulate herself on. Her stubborn elusiveness by day and her bitter attempts to withstand his seduction at night had not turned him from her physically.

She was watering her lush indoor plant collection when he appeared.

'Oh, hello,' she tossed in his general direction, dealing his tall, superbly masculine figure on the threshold the most sparing acknowledgement. But the inescapable weakness a glimpse of him always brought was invading her body, pulling every tiny muscle taut with sharp awareness.

She didn't hear him cross the carpet. The first she knew of it, the dainty watering can was wrested from her and her feet were leaving the floor. He crushed her mouth under his, his tongue thrusting a fierce passage between her yielding lips with a passionate, searing urgency that currented through her with a lightning-bolt efficiency.

'Hello...Polly,' he derided.

Giddily recovering, she shrieked, 'Put me down this minute!'

'As you put the phone down on me yesterday?' he gritted.

She was totally unprepared for the towering rage which made a mask of his darkly handsome visage. 'I didn't put it down. I was about to get in the bath, and I told you that!' she argued, breathlessly involved in a struggle for release that was as undignified as it was unsuccessful.

Her eyes flew wide as Raschid kicked open the door of their bedroom.

'And that... it came before me?'

'Everything comes before you!'

'I will teach you manners if it is the last thing I do,' he swore, dropping her from a height down on to the mercifully well sprung bed.

Polly bounced back against the headboard, her green eyes ablaze, maddened by his treatment. 'You touch me now and I'll never forgive you for it!'

He sent the door crashing shut with a powerful hand and swung round. 'I hear and I tremble,' he scorned. 'The next time I return you will be waiting for me.'

'Behind the door with a brick, in all likelihood!' she snapped.

'And you will have something more to say to me than "Oh, hello",' he mimicked, and yanked off the gold *agal*, a predatory glitter illuminating his wrathful stare. 'What fashion is that in which to greet your husband? You have sulked long enough. I won't stand another day of it!'

'I don't sulk!'

He sauntered over to the bed like a sleek cat stalking an already cornered prey and calmly began to remove his clothes. 'I am master in my own household.'

'You can't do this to me!' she raged, violently thrown by his sudden unforewarned change of tactics.

He lowered his lean, sun-darkened body down beside her, pulling her to him with determined hands. His eyes roamed almost savagely over her. 'If it pleases you... I missed you in my bed,' he breathed less roughly. 'Feel your body against mine. It speaks of welcome, and that is what I will have. I think you missed me too.'

'Do cows jump over the moon?'

Disorientatingly laughter tremored through his long, muscular physique, making Polly unbearably aware of his potent masculinity. 'Ah, Polly, what a talent you have for making me laugh when I'm angry! I should have lost my temper with you long ago.'

There were tears in her eyes. She was trying so desperately hard not to react to him. 'Don't,' she pleaded, fast reaching a stage where she was no longer too proud to plead.

Raschid's lips whispered provocatively over hers. 'You want me,' he murmured, 'and there is no shame in that. For five days all I have thought about is this moment and the pleasure we will share.'

And this was now and tomorrow was another day. That insidious philosophy suppressed that terrible, aching despair, and she surrendered as she had feared she would all along. Five days stretched out over aimless hours and lonely nights could be a lifetime.

'I think cows do jump over the moon.' Raschid's slumbrous gaze tracked mockingly over her when all passion was spent.

They didn't, they went into orbit. Shifting away from him, she fiercely denied that misleading after-intimacy of togetherness and muttered venomously, 'When I'm free I could make a fortune selling my story to one of the tabloids. I've got just the title! *I was an Arab sex slave.*'

The lazy arm which had predictably reached out to prevent her retreat tensed. With an appreciative laugh he dipped his mouth to the smooth curve of her pink cheek. 'I think you are as likely to do that, *aziz*, as walk naked down a street.'

Damn you, don't you ever take me seriously?'

'A sense of humour helps.' Coolly employing his superior strength, he turned her back to face him. 'Do I have to repeat what I said earlier? From now on, you behave,' he spelt out.

'I'm not a child!'

Slowly he rested his dishevelled dark head back on the pillow and looked steadily back at her. 'Only children play hide and seek.'

'Because they want to be found,' Polly countered shakily. 'Well, I'm afraid there was no such ego-boosting motivation behind my wish to spend as little time as possible with you. Now if you're...finished...I'm getting up.'

His hands swept up to close round her slender forearms. 'You are not going anywhere, and you will listen to me. Do you think that the ridiculous lengths you have gone to in avoiding me have not aroused comment? Asif has a phrase,' his brilliant blue eyes glittered up into the pale oval of her face, 'fighting dirty...'

The blood rushed hotly to her face. Not once had it occurred to her that her conduct might embarrass him. Stubbornly engaged in what she deemed a private war of survival, she had forgotten the prying eyes and listening ears surrounding them.

'Perhaps you think I enjoy having my father enquire if I cannot control my wife?' An unhidden flash leapt in his eyes. 'He finds it very amusing. I don't, and while an English gentleman might turn the other cheek, I will not. Push me and you will discover that to your satisfaction if not to your pleasure.'

'Let go of me!' Polly breathed.

'Am I hurting you?'

'That's not the point!'

'That is exactly the point,' Raschid overruled. 'I am sorry if I wound your pride, but better that than any more lasting damage.'

She stiffened. 'If you're threatening me with violence...'

His nostrils flared. 'No man who is truly a man needs to hurt a woman to make her see reason. If I have to hold you to make you listen to me, it is because you spend so much time running away from reality,' he asserted drily. 'While you are my wife you will behave as I expect my wife to behave, and whatever differences we have are not to be set up for public debate. Is that understood?'

Polly quivered with temper and chagrin. 'I hate you!'

'That wasn't the question.'

'You lousy bully!'

'A bully would have cut out your tongue and shackled you to the foot of the bed with a chain by now,' a disturbing quirk matched the sudden humour in his eyes, 'but what a very dull life a bully would lead with a Polly cowed into submission! I believe you understand very well what I have said and I don't think you will repeat those errors.'

'I wonder where you get that idea!'

Slowly he smiled. 'It didn't work, did it? And it is not very comfortable to avoid someone all day and then go to bed with them at night. I believe you must now see the point of the relationship I was trying to establish with you, now that it is being made clear that you cannot embarrass me into sending you home.'

Was that what she had been doing? 'You don't want a relationship, you want a bed partner,' she condemned.

Raschid was inexorably drawing her down on top of him. 'If that is true, I have yet to find one. So far I have taken a human sacrifice to bed and awakened to sullen silences—not to mention the disappearing wife act.'

At this Polly's lips opened on a soundless oh of outraged disbelief.

He smiled. 'But I live in hope of the sacrifice becoming a partner.'

'I want to get up!' she repeated unsteadily.

His response was husky and soft. 'Lie to yourself, *aziz*, but never lie to me.'

Her head twisted away. 'I meant what I said.'

Tumbling her over, he smoothly reversed their positions. Gazing down at her, he indolently laced a brown hand into the wild disarray of her bright hair. 'Your obstinacy may rival mine, but not, I think, your endurance. Or your powers of self-denial. Exactly where would you be if I didn't throw you on beds, *aziz*?' he demanded with lethal satire.

Pinpointing her deep sense of floundering inadequacy, he held it ruthlessly up to the light. He hurt her as he had never hurt her before. Her susceptibility to his smallest caress was indefensible. 'You... bastard!' she muttered.

A formidable cool sharded his intent stare. 'Even if I should find adoration distinctly boring, how I dislike to hear such language upon my wife's lips.'

You liar! Did Berah bore you? She was tortured by the memory of the male who had talked of his first wife in a tone the reverential reserved for an early Christian martyr, the male who had sensitively removed to new surroundings to evade distressing reminders. Berah had touched him deeply. Berah had awarded him all that an Arab prince was brought up to expect from a wife—in public and in private. Her love had been acceptable. Her love had been returned. Jealousy laced with pain wrenched at Polly. 'You won't be receiving adoration from me!'

Without hesitation Raschid released her, casting her bewildered face a hard, glittering smile. 'However, there are other things that I will have,' he declared. 'There you are, Polly. Just this once I give you what you say you want—your own company and an empty bed. But why is it, I wonder, that you should lack the glow of a woman receiving her heart's desire?'

Her pallor was pronounced, her pulse suddenly a thunderbeat. Her heart's desire... Oh, lord, help me! she thought. In that bemused instant of savage rejection and jealousy, she saw. She saw what she had blindly fought for and, conversely, blindly fought against. It was not solely that lean, sunbronzed body that roused the indecently insatiable hunger of her senses. No, it was so much more. That quick and clever brain, that potent aura of leashed animal vitality, that quicksilver humour which could flash out disconcertingly from behind the gravity, that... She could have gone on endlessly, a new convert glorifying her idol. She loved him, head over heels over sanity. Logic had nothing to do with it. Love, she appreciated dazedly, wasn't something you could control or decide not to feel.

'Ask me, admit that you want me, and I'll come back to bed.'

Wrenched from stricken self-analysis, she looked at Raschid weakly. Oh, why does it have to be you? she thought. A lithe, unashamed pagan, already provocatively aware of his physical power over her. She recognised that change in him—that overt, predatory awareness of his sexual magnetism. She could have sworn that it hadn't always been there. But it must have been. Wasn't blindness one of her worst failings? And wasn't perception his strongest talent? How long would it be before he guessed that this wasn't the full extent of his power?

In the silence he sent her a wolfish smile, amused now, outrageously confident. With it went a look of outright possession. 'It may not be today, it may not even be tomorrow, but you will make that admission eventually,' he told her.

'I hope you have the patience of Job!' The snappy retort came to her with the saving ease of habit, but he left her sunk in depression.

Even desire didn't threaten his cool self-dominion. He was as content to sate his high sex drive with Polly as he would have been with a mistress. He was just as safe from emotional involvement. All this fine-sounding talk about wanting to establish a relationship was a subtle counter-manoeuvre aimed at driving her metaphorically to her knees and moulding her into the required image of wifely behaviour.

It wasn't worth any more than that wretched swimming pool being created for the past ten days at phenomenal expense and incredible noise out in their courtyard. Had she asked for a swimming pool? Even hinted? It was pretty hard to pretend that you didn't notice a swimming pool being built, but Polly had managed the feat. And now in the midst of a running battle she discovered that she didn't want to fight Raschid any longer, but she shrank from the danger of him realising how she really felt about him.

In the middle of the night the call came, shrilling through the veil of her slumber, causing her to mutter crossly, but late phone calls for Raschid were not unusual.

'I'll take this on another line.' Before she drifted back to sleep, she wondered that he should have spoken in English.

It was still dark when he shook her awake. He was fully dressed, his features tautly cast. He gripped her hand firmly, his eyes were steady. 'You must be brave, *aziz*,' he urged. 'I have bad news to relate. Your father has had a heart attack—a serious one. He is in intensive care.'

'No!' Her mind rejected it entirely. Her energetic, jovial father, lying on the boundary between life and death? Impossible! But beneath Raschid's level gaze, she lost that fragile, futile confidence. 'Dear heaven!' she whispered.

'As soon as you are dressed we will be on our way to England. Zenobia has already packed for you, the arrangements are made. I didn't wish to waken you before it was necessary.'

Polly gasped, 'That call... it was for me! Mother...'

Raschid sighed. 'It was not from Anthea. It was Mrs King, the housekeeper, who contacted me. Your sister Maggie also spoke briefly to me. I understand that your mother is so distraught that she is in bed under sedation. Your family are greatly in need of you.'

Her mother had collapsed—of course she had. She had always leant heavily on her husband. With his life in the balance, she would go to pieces, regardless of how that reaction would affect her family. 'The children must be terribly frightened,' she muttered worriedly.

'Quite so, and though it is very hard for you, that is why you must be strong—for all their sakes. Your father is alive,' he emphasised. 'Hold to that. He has tremendous zest for life, and that must be in his favour.'

They landed to a grey, wet London evening. The waiting car ferried them the hundred miles to the local hospital, where the consultant was carefully non-committal. There was, they learnt, a danger of a second attack. Polly was allowed to glance in at her sleeping father. His ruddy face was drained and caved in. She rammed back an undisciplined sob of fear as Raschid's arm moved bracingly round her. He had been so marvellous, immensely calm and reassuring and sensible. It was second nature for him to advocate the setting aside of personal feelings to consider others more vulnerable.

Maggie rushed down the steps of the house and flung herself into Polly's arms. The household was in chaos. 'Why couldn't Uncle Peter and Aunt Janice have been here?' she sobbed. 'Mummy thinks Daddy's going to die!'

Polly also regretted the absence of Chris's parents. Had they been in England they would have come to Anthea's assistance, but they were in South America where Peter Jeffries, a high-flying executive for an international consortium, was engaged on important business. They weren't free to fly home to support Anthea through her ordeal, and Polly sighed, fearing that her mother would find her presence of little comfort.

The following days were ever after a blur for Polly. A flood of well-wishers, denied access at the hospital, called at the house. Anthea exhausted Polly with her constant demands for reassurance and her pettish refusals to accept it. Her visits to her husband's bedside always resulted in an emotional breakdown when she came home again. Unable as she was to accept a female in a supportive role, the task of soothing Anthea fell upon Raschid. His phenomenal patience with her mother's hysteria shamed Polly. In her heart she knew that he deemed Anthea a pretty, self-orientated and utterly useless woman, who was failing her children at a time when they most needed her.

On the same day that the consultant cautiously pronounced that Ernest appeared to be out of immediate danger, Raschid was recalled to the Middle East by an attack on a Dhareini tanker in the Gulf. Polly was in the nursery, where she had been spending most of her time trying to keep up her siblings' spirits. She was reading a story to Elaine with Timothy sleepily curled up on her lap when Raschid came to break the news to her.

In the dull glow of the gas fire his constraint was noticeable. Putting Timothy into Maggie's reluctant arms, she followed Raschid from the room. 'Many casualties?' she asked.

'The number is not yet certain.' His angular cheekbones stood out in sharp relief. 'They have been airlifted to the nearest hospital. I am afraid that this means that I must leave.'

'Of course. Those poor men . . . their families.' Polly's voice broke, and shamefully it was not out of shocked compassion alone. For a selfish moment, she could not bear the knowledge that they were to be separated.

Timothy's cantankerous wails flooded the landing as Maggie flounced out. 'He just won't settle for me. He wants you.' Uncomfortably she glanced between Polly and Raschid, for they were several feet apart.

Her brother fastened chubby arms victoriously round her neck and subsided. Over the top of his curly head, Polly took in Raschid's absorption in a section of un-adorned wall and the rigidity of his profile. He really was upset. In fact, she had never seen him so upset about anything that he wouldn't even look at her.

'It may also be some time before I can return,' he related woodenly. 'Excuse me, I must take my leave of your mother.'

Her heart was heavy as lead. Mrs King was packing for him, and she insisted on helping. When she came down to the hall Raschid was leaving the drawing-room. She could not help but feel neglected at the inordinately long time he had devoted to her mother while she had wasted time upstairs, believing he would return there.

'I must go now.'

Uncertainly she drew level with him. He inclined his dark head, a silvered coolness in the scrutiny he sent fleetingly over her. 'I will keep in touch,' he told her.

'I'll miss you.' It was dragged from her.

He elevated an ebony brow. 'I think you have much to keep you occupied here.'

And that was that. He strode out of the door, down the steps and into the car. He didn't touch her. He didn't look back once. He took his leave of her with no more emotion than he would have used with a servant. He left her behind, and she was white-faced and sick inside. He made her painfully conscious that, for all his patience and kindness, he had not even kissed her since they left Dharein. Generally she had been too tired and too busy to refine too much on that restraint. But once or twice, yearning for that comfort that only intimacy with a loved one could bring, Polly had been very tempted to drop hints—only to be forestalled by the embarrassing fact that she didn't know how to be subtle or even clumsy in that direction when Mrs King had put them in a room with single beds.

She pressed a shaking hand to her lips. They had had so little time here alone together; she had spent long hours with the children to keep them from under her mother's feet. Raschid hadn't come looking for her, though. In retrospect it seemed to her now as if he had been steadily withdrawing from her ever since they arrived.

'Really, darling,' snapped Anthea when her daughter reached for a second scone, 'I'm not surprised you're putting on weight!'

Encountering Janice Jeffries' sympathetic eyes, Polly flushed. 'Actually I've lost some,' she said.

'Nonsense! The buttons on that blouse are pulling.' An astonishingly coy look banished her mother's irritation. 'That was always my first sign. Don't be prissy, Polly. Are you pregnant? You can tell me—I am your mother.'

Freezing, Polly studied her plate. 'No, I'm not.'

'Then I suggest you cut out the sweet things.' In disappointment Anthea became sharp.

Janice, whose weekend stay was due to conclude that afternoon, tactfully turned the conversation. 'I understand that you're leaving on Thursday, Polly.'

Anthea sniffed, 'Everybody's abandoning me!'

Chris's mother laughed. 'Ernest will be home on Tuesday and Peter and I will be down the weekend after next. Polly must be missing her husband. She'll soon have been here a month.'

Anthea frowned. 'Good lord, is it really that long?'

Leaving the two older women chatting, Polly went for a walk outside. In two weeks it would be Christmas. It was very cold. She dug her hands into the pockets of the old coat she had taken from the gunroom. The emergency here was over; it was her own personal crisis that raged on. Raschid hadn't phoned in five days. Contact had slowly wound down in frequency as her father's health steadily improved. Raschid had not once prompted her return. She had finally made her own arrangements. She would just darned well turn up—Hey, remember me, I'm your wife!

Her strained face convulsed and suddenly she was crying. It was happening just as he had said it would happen. Her attraction had faded. Raschid might not be ready to think of divorce yet, but he was in no hurry to reclaim her. When she heard steps behind her, she stiffened in dismay.

'I thought I'd give our mothers an extension before I broke up the party,' teased Chris as he drew level. He peered at Polly's turned-away profile. 'Here, what's wrong?'

In embarrassment she shook her head, praying that he would leave her alone again. On his couple of visits to Ladybright before his parents' return from abroad, she had been uneasily conscious of his searching glances, his efforts to take their conversations into more personal channels. But some things weren't for sharing. One of them was the conviction that Raschid was making the most out of a cast-iron excuse for their separation. Even his father could not question a daughter's attendance on a sick parent.

'It's that damned odd marriage of yours, isn't it?' he persisted curtly.

A choked sob escaped her. When she would have turned away, he prevented her by closing his arms round her. 'Oh, Chris, don't be nice,' she begged. 'It'll only make me worse.'

His hold tightened uncomfortably. 'He can't force you to go back to him!'

'But I want to go back,' Polly said in surprise.

'You don't need to pretend with me.' As he stared into her lovely, tear-drenched eyes, his features tightened. 'Polly, I ...'

'I'm not pretending.' Her hand was braced against his shoulder, trying to press him back. Even as she dazedly read his intent expression, it was too late. He was kissing her. For a stunned second she was still before she jerked her head angrily back. 'For goodness' sake, Chris!'

Abashed and awkward now, he let out a groan. 'Hell, I'm sorry. I got a bit carried away.'

In her high heels she could see over his shoulder. A hundred yards away beneath the trees lining the rear entrance to the estate, a dark male figure was stationary. In bemused horror Polly blinked. Raschid was already swinging away to retrace his steps. Her pulses had no time to go off on the Big Dipper ride he usually inspired.

'I could kill you!' she launched fiercely at Chris before she set off across the sodden lawn in pursuit. When she breathlessly reached the driveway, the silver limousine was still parked. Raschid was lodged by the open rear door, darkly magnificent in a navy suit and inhumanly still.

'You will have your divorce,' he pronounced flatly.

The cold menace of his chilling stare killed the words of explanation bubbling on her lips, and when she moved forward, he slashed a hand through the air, forcing her to a halt. 'Do not return to Dharein. I will neither see you nor speak with you again.'

The blazing, earth-shattering row Polly had anticipated was nowhere in sight. Tried and sentenced without a hearing and dismissed with a snap of his aristocratic fingers, she was in shock. Before she could recover, Raschid slid into the car and slammed the door. Her eyes were maintaining a glazed contact with the receding car when Chris reached for her. Raschid hadn't even been angry enough to lose his head, she was thinking numbly.

Possibly he had seen what he wanted to see—the excuse to end their marriage.

'Polly, I don't know what to say,' Chris muttered tightly. 'Ever since your wedding, when I realised you weren't a kid any more, I guess I've had this feeling that I missed the boat, but I didn't mean to come on to you. Holding you like that . . . well, you're very tempting and I just lost my head for a moment.'

Barely listening, she mumbled, 'It's not contagious.'

Anger flared briefly within her. Had Raschid no faith in her at all? No trust? No respect? If only she had slapped Chris like some outraged Victorian maiden! Raschid had been too far away to see her annoyance, hear her angry words.

'What are you going to do?' Chris pressed. 'I feel terrible. This is my fault.'

Polly shrugged jerkily. 'It's just a stupid storm in a teacup. Forget about it,' she advised tautly. 'I'm flying back in a few days anyway.'

He sighed. 'If there's anything I can . . .'

'Nothing.'

'How do you intend to cover his departure?'

'I don't think he'd entered the house and the car was parked out of view. He could see us from here,' she pointed out, tight-mouthed. Raschid had spied on them, he hadn't advertised his presence, and what had he been doing arriving by the back entrance? A kiss, and she was in the **div**orce court. How dared he condemn her out of hand!

Stalking through the front door, she walked into a bower of flowers. Maggie got up from amongst the beribboned baskets of white roses. 'These came half an hour ago. Aren't they gorgeous? Raschid does have style.'

'Raschid sent them?' Polly gulped, and swallowed. If Chris hadn't been standing there guiltily ill at ease, she would have sobbed her heart out in absolute despair. It

was incredibly hard now to recall that she had once believed she loved Chris.

'Who else?' Maggie eyed her sister's drawn pallor
curiously. 'He may not phone much, but he knows how
to employ the language of flowers!'

'If everyone would remain seated please,' the stewardess
called unexpectedly while Polly was trying to don her
*aba* without elbowing the passenger beside her.

'Is this lady... Her Highness?'

As Polly triumphed over the *aba* she recognised Seif
and Raoul, dwarfing the stewardess in the aisle. Startled,
she stared. Both men bowed low, then Seif motioned a
hand. Why were Raschid's bodyguards collecting her off
her commercial flight? He hadn't tried to prevent her
return, and she had clung feverishly to that favourable
omission. She had phoned the palace. Medir had told
her that Raschid was unavailable. Pressed pitilessly on
a third call, he had revealed that Raschid was in the desert
at some place called Jebel Kaddish. Polly had duly announced her arrival time at Jumani airport.

Outside the heat of midday engulfed her. 'Where are
we going?' she asked.

'To the plane.'

'We've just got off the plane!'

No answer. Her anxiety level was reaching el-
ephantine proportions. They led her on a long trudge
round the airport buildings. A curious little craft sat
there, a cross between a helicopter and a seaplane without
floats.

'I wish to go to the palace,' Polly declared tautly.

'Princess go join Prince Raschid.' Seif made idiotic
stepping motions into the empty cargo hold facing her,
much as though he was trying to coax a bashful sheep
into a truck. 'Long flight, must leave... pronto,' he produced with a gold-capped grin.

She boarded with her case. Where her wishes ran contrary to Raschid's Seif and Raoul became uniformly deaf. A rough bench seat adorned by an incongruous cushion was indicated by the pilot. The two guards remained on the tarmac. Raschid was still in the desert. Did he want to see her somewhere more private than the palace? Or did that whistling pilot have instructions to push her out without a parachute above cloud cover? Polly, get a grip on yourself, she told herself. You're facing a battle royal, not an execution!

# CHAPTER EIGHT

WITHOUT a view the flight was endless. The pilot chain-smoked, making conditions doubly unpleasant. When they landed Polly stumbled gratefully out into the open air. The plane was overhung by a massive black outcrop of jagged rock that protruded like broken teeth into the sky. It screened them from even a whisper of a breeze in the intense heat. Jebel Kaddish was a desolate landmark, surrounded by a barbarously bleak and magnificent landscape of dunes. In the changing light the sands gradually shaded from beige to ochre as they marched in undulating succession into the horizon.

A shout burst from the pilot and Polly spun round. She had to shade her eyes to see the tribesmen, precariously perched on camels, travelling towards them at speed. The dust they were churning up almost obliterated her glimpse of the rider on the black stallion in their midst. As they approached they spread out and finally reined in, encircling the plane. Steady-eyed Bedouin with thin, weathered faces, they were a ragged collection, yet they possessed the intrinsic dignity of a proud people in their erect carriage.

Marzouk pranced, reacting to his rider's fierce tension. Burningly blue eyes slammed into hers. Beneath the *aba* she couldn't breathe; she couldn't break that savage stare either. The pilot broke it, hurrying forward to bow low and engage with gusto on the ritual and lengthy greetings that betrayed his desert origins. Mortified by Raschid's failure to acknowledge her, Polly studied the ground with burning cheeks.

A tribesman dismounted and took her case to strap it on to a lone baggage camel while a second led another camel forward and with a practised flick of his cane made it kneel. On its back it bore a basketwork litter draped with bright cloth. Raschid at last walked Marzouk over to her and sprang down.

'Look, I didn't expect a welcome mat, but——' she began huskily.

Without a word he scooped her up and settled her into the litter, indifferent to the ill-tempered camel's vicious attempts to snap at him. His prompt response to his wife's reluctance provoked many covert smiles, and Polly's anxious eyes brightened with indignation.

The camel lumbered upright and the world lurched sickeningly. As they moved off at a steady pace, the swaying movements of the litter sentenced her to motion sickness. It was some time before she realised that by relaxing her body and keeping her attention off ground level, she could banish it. By then the only sounds were the crunching footfalls of the four-legged beasts of burden and the riotous clamour of her own heartbeat.

They came upon the camp suddenly over a rise, a cluster of around twenty black tents and bush fires sending up smoking grey spirals. Darkness was falling now with astonishing speed and her muscles ached in every joint. The logic behind bringing her here evaded her, but she was very grateful that the journey was over.

As she clambered stiffly from the litter, two manservants she recognised from the palace bowed low. Raschid trailed her unceremoniously past them into the shadowy depths of the nearest tent and pressed her round behind an interior wall of intricate leather and beadwork. Rugs and quilts were heaped there on a low rope bed, and she sat down immediately. Her legs were shaky supports.

'Remove the *aba*. Only the elderly women mask their faces here.'

Obeying, Polly glanced up, wet tendrils of hair clinging to her brow. And neither the searing intensity of his stare nor his dangerous stillness could quell the treacherous rush of excitement seizing her. It was a dark enchantment that stripped her of pride and principle. If she had ever been strong with Raschid, she had never been weaker than she was now. The silence tortured her. 'Say something!'

A lean hand clenched to show the white of bone. 'Keep yourself from my sight!' he said icily.

She scrambled up, blocking his exit. 'At least hear what I have to say!'

'Cry it to the wind. You are as likely to hear an answer there,' he gritted in caustic derision. 'With every hour that passes you will regret the insolence and the false confidence which encouraged you to disobey me.'

A creature recognition of cold threat enforced her retreat. And he was gone in a flicker of movement with the soundless grace of a hunting animal. Nervously Polly looked around. Her surroundings were basic. She was not surprised. The servants were a necessary sacrifice to status, but Raschid wouldn't flaunt his wealth here. In a corner she espied a radio apparatus and two elaborate bronze oil lamps. Beyond the dividing wall she found tinned goods and sacks and a second doorway. She knew that the very front section of the tent was reserved for the all-male bastion of the traditional coffee hearth where the men entertained. From outside drifted the aromatic enticement of cooking food.

He couldn't ignore her presence indefinitely, could he? Yet he must want to do just that. The most expensive bride in the Middle East had given the poorest satisfaction. In one way or another she had fought him every day of their marriage. He could have strung her along, he could have pretended it was forever and by now she would have been eating out of his hand. But while she acted on her emotions, Raschid acted according to his principles. He would not have lied to her.

How much had her bloody-minded behaviour before he saw her in Chris's arms contributed to his distrust? Oh, how childish she had been! Out of her depth and trying to keep her head above water, she had used the only means of defiance at her disposal. In some ways, she acknowledged unhappily, it had almost been a game to her while she tried to raise a real live emotional reaction from Raschid. But where did all that inappropriate groundwork leave her now? He didn't want her here. So what's new, Polly...? Her thoughts were bitter. But he would believe her, surely he would? If he didn't... no, she refused even to think of that eventuality. This was just a stupid storm in a teacup, she reminded herself. It was just that he hadn't realised the fact yet.

Mahmoud brought her a savoury meat and rice concoction and a frothy cup of milk, and she ate hungrily. He reappeared with a shallow dish of water in which she was evidently expected to wash. Doing her best, she dressed again, frowning over the tightness of her waistband. Her mother was right and the scales were wrong. She was putting on weight. As a long shadow darkened the magazine she had taken out to read, she glanced up apprehensively.

'You should be in bed. Before dawn we break camp.'

'Can we talk now?' Already Raschid was removing his clothes in quiet, economic movements.

'I have no desire to talk.' In the soft light shadows obscured his expression.

Tension formed an iron band across her temples. She had already opened her case, but little within was suitable for a desert sojourn. What might have been comfortable would not be deemed respectable among nomads, whose women were shapelessly if colourfully covered from head to toe. Pulling out a lawn nightdress, Polly hesitated, her fingers coiled tight in the fabric. 'I was crying and he was comforting me. He kissed me...I didn't kiss him.'

He grated an Arabic profanity, his teeth a feral white slash against his sunbronzed features. Frustration and strain summoned tears to her eyes. Granted more privacy than tent walls, she would have dared his anger and persisted. Edgily she began to undress again. Never had she been more conscious of Raschid, never had skin seemed more indecently naked.

Impatient fingers wrenched the nightdress from her grasp and flung it aside before she could drop it over her head. As she collided in shock with incandescently blue eyes, the brand of fear she could taste flooded her mouth. 'No...!' she shuddered in stricken understanding.

Raschid doused the lamps, plunging them into darkness. He found her with ease. There was no place to go, no room for evasive action, and if she cried out, the whole camp would hear her. Whatever she did, it would not turn Raschid from his cruel purpose. He was in the merciless grip of a murderous rage which had smouldered unabated for over five days. The icy mask of disdain he had shown her at Ladybright had been a façade, no more indicative of his real feelings than a smile would have been.

He laced a hard hand into the silken fall of her hair. 'Let me show you how I would treat a whore,' he invited with soft, biting menace. 'If I thought of you as my wife, I would kill you with my bare hands. Yes, you succeeded, *aziz*. Celebrate your hour of victory now, for the glory will be brief. You twisted my guts with jealousy, and for that education, I am ungrateful.'

'There's nothing between Chris and...' His hand clamped over her lips.

'I doubt if he'll want you back when I am finished with you. That lingering and so appealing innocence of yours will be gone. And then he would have to wait a very long time. For as long as it amuses me you will remain in Dharein, and when I wish, I will lie with you,' he swore with muted savagery. 'You have no rights. I grant you none, and I thank you for revealing your true self. I have you on my terms now, and I will yield you no quarter.'

Polly was paralysed by the raw force of his invective. A sleeping tiger had been kicked into wakefulness and uncaged. She had yearned for the power to pierce his detachment, but not with the violent, destructive drive of emotions that had splintered his control. For that sin and for this vengeful act of subjugation he intended, Raschid would never forgive her. He would despise himself for using force with a defenceless woman. Her brain functioned frantically as he joined her, his lean body achingly familiar, but the hands sweeping her shrinking flesh were coolly set to shame, not to pleasure.

'I . . . I need to go . . . outside,' she stammered in desperation.

Releasing his breath in a hiss, he folded back. Barely able to credit the success of her gambit, Polly blindly fumbled for some clothing and footwear, pulling on what she suspected was his discarded woollen *tobe*.

'Don't get lost.'

For once, intuition was letting him down. Until he cooled off, Polly had no other objective inside her panic-stricken head. Raschid was not presently accessible to reasoned persuasion.

Fortunately their tent was set some distance from the others near the edge of the camp. As a dog barked she quickened her step. Her energy level was on an adrenalin boost. Moonlight cast a black and white photographic clarity on the desert, and she ran like the wind. Glancing back to check that her flight had gone unnoticed, she hurried on again without looking—and stepped into mid-air. She went head over heels down a slope that had lain concealed by shadow, sand gritting her mouth and her nose, but she didn't cry out. At the bottom, winded, she got up and shook herself, her heart thumping fit to burst.

It seemed common sense to travel along the meandering valley of low ground between the dunes rather than exhaust herself trying to climb. Besides, she wasn't planning on straying too far. The air was surprisingly humid, lacking the frost she had expected, and she settled into a half trotting, half walking pace in the eerie, supernatural quiet. Raschid would look for her, and by the time he found her—lord knows, a herd of camels couldn't have left clearer tracks—she prayed that he would have calmed down. Should anyone else be involved in her disappearance, he could say that she had lost her bearings. Nobody would suspect that it hadn't been an accident. Well, what else could she have done?

Raschid was half out of his mind with jealousy. A dark, profoundly sexual jealousy, new to his experience, had ripped the lid off his outer skin of cool to reveal the passionate turbulence of the emotions beneath, and the strength of those emotions had shattered her. If he had felt like that, why had he left her with Chris in England?

Without warning the entire surrealistic landscape around her was brilliantly illuminated by a forked flash of lightning. A fine mist of sand sprayed her shocked face as a wind came up out of nowhere and the first drops of rain sprinkled down. Above her the black velvet heavens were suddenly ripped asunder by spearing arrows of blinding light that jetted down into the ground with a ferocity that terrified her. Like a strobe disco display magnified a thousand times, the elements began to go mad.

The rain now fell in a lashing blast, plastering fabric wetly to her limbs, stinging her exposed skin. Instinctively she crouched down, trying to protect herself from the incredibly heavy downpour. When an animal leapt at her, she was knocked flat, and since she hadn't seen what had attacked her, she screamed so loudly that she hurt her throat. The dog stood over her whining, while its panting mate raced up and licked at her hand.

Raschid barked a command and the dogs retreated. The noise of the thumping rain prevented Polly from hearing what he slung at her. Water streamed down his face as he lifted her and practically threw her up on to Marzouk's back. Her instant of unholy relief at first sight of him was limited by the realisation that he had put his saluki hounds on her trail. He had hunted her down like an animal.

It was a nightmare trek back to the camp. Her teeth chattered convulsively, her skin numb from a cold that penetrated to her bones. Raschid had to carry her into the tent.

'If I took a whip to you now, no man would blame me!' he roared at her above the storm. Ablaze with dark fury, he dropped down to strip the sodden *tobe* from her shivering limbs.

'You put dogs on me, you brute!' she gasped.

He produced a towel and began to rub it roughly over every complaining, squirming inch of her. As her circulation revived, the exercise became painful. Unsympathetically he glowered at her. 'What were you waiting out there for?' he demanded. 'Noah's Ark? You lie in a *shoeb* . . . a dry torrent bed. Didn't you see the water pooling? Within minutes it would have flooded. In winter there are flash floods in the desert. My own people have drowned. The storms come suddenly and it's not always possible to reach higher ground!'

'Stop shouting!' she begged.

He rolled her dexterously into a quilt and tugging her forward, towelled dry her dripping hair. 'Another few minutes and the salukis would have lost your scent in the rain,' he bit out rawly. 'You could have died. Your tracks would have been washed away and the sands above you would have slipped down to conceal your body.

Allah be praised that you are saved and that no man lost his life in pursuing the most stupid, reckless...' At that point words seemed to fail him and he subsided. Rain-washed violet eyes framed by spiky wet lashes surveyed her pallor with grim satisfaction.

In the electric silence, he slowly breathed in and screened his eyes. 'I shout at you, but the blame is mine,' he asserted in a roughened undertone. 'In threatening you, I have shamed myself more than you have shamed me in the arms of your lover.'

Polly's eyes ached. Her hand crept up uncertainly on to the brown fingers resting tautly on his thighs. 'He's not my lover—I was telling the truth. It was an emotional moment and Chris made a mistake,' she cited unsteadily. 'But if you won't believe me, if you won't listen, what more can I do to convince you?'

Raschid's hard-set profile was unresponsive. He looked at her small hand and it retreated immediately. He got up. 'You should not have returned,' he said very quietly. 'But what choice had you? I placed you in an intolerable position with your family.'

'Where are you going?'

'I must attend to Marzouk.' He vanished back out into the slackening rain before she could utter the heresy that his horse was more expendable than he was and he was still soaking wet.

An opportunity to vent some of his pent-up anger had made him more approachable, and even in anger he had automatically taken care of her needs. What agonised her was the suspicion that, guilty or innocent, she was no more welcome. Then that scarcely fitted his behaviour. Jealousy suggested... what? Caring? She grimaced. It was more likely to be the reaction of a very possessive male, enraged by the slur on his masculinity and the insult to his pride. He had walked away from her in England. Yet he had arrived that day with flowers and an evident intent to surprise her. It didn't make sense.

To say the very least, Raschid's behaviour had been erratic since they had received the news of her father's heart attack. Then, when he had talked of a more normal relationship, he had withdrawn from her in every way. He had stayed away, maintaining a contact of skeletal cool... and then the flowers. If there was an explicable pattern there, Polly was darned if she could see it.

She wakened to grey light and the bloodcurdling roar of an angry camel. Around her the covers were undisturbed. Raschid hadn't slept beside her. As soon as she sat up, a slender Bedouin girl appeared with water for her to wash. She must have been sitting outside the tent listening for the first sound. Giggling shyly at Polly's halting attempts to communicate, she gave her name as Hirfa. It took considerable dumbshow to request her need for a pair of scissors. Polly put on her loosest dress and then cut the top off the *aba*, dropping the butchered garment over her shoulders to cover her bare legs. She was pleased to have solved the clothing problem so easily.

When she finally left the tent, half a dozen chattering women converged on it. The camp had almost vanished but for the tent roof under which Raschid's oversleeping wife had rested. The men were congregated round the fires drinking tea in relaxation while their wives and daughters laboured to pack every possession.

Nearby Raschid lifted a hand, motioning Polly over. 'Join us,' he invited. 'Do you want some tea?'

In some surprise she sank down beside him. His companions were noticeably quiet at the unconventional development. 'It's cool, isn't it?' she remarked, a conversational opener that only had Mahmoud dispatched to fetch her a rug she didn't need.

At Raschid's signal, the teamaker served her first with the next round. Smiles were in evidence as Raschid said something.

'What did you say?' Polly wanted to know.

'Never mind. You are accepted because I accept you here.'

Acceptance was a dubious honour. The strong tea, thick with sugar, was served without milk and most of the men were smoking. The fumes were taxing on her sensitive stomach, and she dimly wondered why; smoke had never bothered her until recently. But, listening to the melodic rise and fall of voices, a kind of peace embraced her. The confrontation over, perhaps the talking would come soon.

'I thought desert travel was all down to trucks these days,' she confided when some of the men had drifted away.

'This is deep dune country,' Raschid explained. 'The four-wheel-drive which may traverse this terrain has not yet been invented, and even if it was, these Bedouin could not afford it. There are no roads in the interior—the sands would soon swallow them up. In summer when the tribe stay by the borewells they use old trucks to transport water to their livestock, but they leave them with settled relatives or sell them when it is time for the winter migration. I agree that this background is not for you.'

Polly tensed. 'I didn't mean that.'

He shrugged. 'At this time of year I usually spend some time in the desert. When we had been apart for so long, I could not let you return to the palace.'

'I'm quite happy here,' she assured him.

'Conditions are spartan,' he said flatly.

'I don't mind.' Polly was starting to get annoyed.

His narrowed eyes rested on her. 'Perhaps I do.'

'Perhaps you just don't want me here!'

He sighed. 'You are over-sensitive this morning, and that is also my fault.' He sprang up and moved a rueful hand. 'Everyone awaits us.'

Cocooned back within the litter, she reflected on his calm, uninformative manner. Was he thinking over what she had said? Having mastered his temper, was he now seeing reason? At least he was speaking to her again. Great, Polly, you can read a lot into that, she thought. Why aren't you angry with him? You have every right to be angry.

The long, winding cavalcade trailed steadily out into the desert wastes. As the burning crimson orb of the sun ascended, the brilliance of the colours shed on the sands fascinated her. Occasionally strange formations of volcanic rock interrupted the vast landscape, but as the sun reached its zenith, the glare sapped the earth beneath of life. Polly was nearly asleep sitting up when the caravan came to a sluggish halt.

Moving her cramped limbs was agony, and Raschid came to her assistance. As his arms released her, her head swam dizzily. Everything blurred into formless shades of grey and she passed out cold.

Woozily meeting the stark azure eyes above hers, she mumbled, 'I'm sorry, I just don't know what...'

The concern harshening his features eased. 'This journey is too taxing for you.'

An improvised shelter had been erected to provide her with shade. Self-pity overcame her and the tears welled up. She was hot and sweaty and miserable, and Raschid was giving her a look that said she must have been feeling ill to faint and why hadn't she mentioned it sooner? But she hadn't been feeling ill.

'Don't cry. Of all the female weapons I abhor, tears are the most unfair,' he muttered. 'And it is worse that it is not a weapon with you.'

Since there wasn't a weapon in her armoury that she wouldn't use to hang on to him, the exasperating gush continued. What was wrong with her? Of late she had emulated a wet weekend all too often and all too easily.

'Polly... I beg of you.' Presented with a tissue, she guiltily mopped up.

Unnerved by the brooding gravity of his appraisal, she looked away, and he sighed. 'In marrying you I have caused you great unhappiness.' His deep, dark drawl was very low-pitched. 'Sometimes, as the sun at noon, you can make me a little crazy...or a lot crazy, like last night. Unlike you, I do not share my feelings easily, and some, believe me, are more wisely kept private. But I must ask your pardon for doubting your loyalty. I did not have sufficient cause to condemn you unheard.'

She was weighted by the funereal atmosphere. 'It's forgotten,' she hastened to tell him.

'You are too forgiving. I have not treated you as I promised.'

Polly had to gulp inelegantly into the tissue to fend off another flood. By then Raschid was already rising and helping her up. 'The tent is prepared and you must rest. I had hoped that today we might travel on to Aldeza, but you are too tired. You have still to sleep off your jetlag.'

'What's at Aldeza?'

He said something in incomprehensible Arabic and his mouth tightened wryly. 'The Palace of the Fountains. You will be comfortable there at least.'

She awoke to soft, artificial light. Once more Hirfa magically appeared. Unfortunately Polly couldn't understand what the girl was asking her and she left again. When she returned with Raschid, Polly was wretchedly conscious of her bedraggled appearance.

'Hirfa wishes to know if you want a bath,' he explained.

'A bath?' she echoed.

He laughed huskily. 'We are near a well. I bathed earlier. Even if the legendary luxury of an Arab prince's desert dwelling must fall far short of popular and romantic expectation,' he added wryly, 'at least you may be clean.'

An antiquated tin bath was carted in. It took buckets and buckets of lightly steaming water to fill it. Embarrassed by the labour involved, Polly only stopped feeling conscience-stricken when she was free to luxuriate in water for once more than an inch deep. It was heavenly! She thought of Raschid's smile, his laughter. Later, she mused dizzily, with a wicked little shiver of anticipation, later he would make love to her. Even as she dried herself, her skin moistened and her cheeks warmed. She was a prey to the thousand erotic images imprinted on her memory bank.

But dinner was not to be the cosy twosome she had innocently pictured. After helping her to dress, Hirfa ushered her outside. In the centre of the camp, a large fire was burning. Round it the men were gathered. On its environs the womenfolk were cooking on small fires and in between the children were running about, noisy in their excitement.

As she settled beside Raschid he explained that since they were leaving the camp in the morning, he was playing host to thank the Bedouin for their hospitality. Private conversation was impossible, and when the men rested back to smoke and recite the long, tall stories and legends that richly endowed their spoken heritage, Polly bowed out, recognising that her presence was acting as something of a dampener. She drifted back to the tent and got ready for bed.

It was ages before Raschid followed suit. Shyly she kept her eyes closed while he undressed. When he slid in beside her, the minutes slowly passed and he made no move to touch her. She had feigned sleep too well.

'I'm awake,' she muttered, then flushed.

'Count chickens,' he advised shortly.

'It's sheep, not chickens.'

'Sleep, Polly.' The message was succinct.

Rejection bit deep. Although pride urged her to silence, she could not maintain it. 'Are you still suspicious about Chris?' she asked him.

'No.'

Stiff with hurt and bewilderment, she whispered, 'Then why——?'

In the gloom Raschid moved. A match was struck and a lamp shed unwelcome clarity on her hot face. 'It is wiser this way.'

Stunned, she dropped her head. 'Yet when I wanted it this way, you wouldn't hear of it.'

'I was wrong.' He seemed to be measuring his words carefully, and well he might have done, for her temper was starting to rise. 'I am not afraid to admit myself at fault. The money...it was less than nothing to me. I should have let you sleep alone. I won't take advantage of you in that fashion again.'

Evading visual contact, Polly bit her lower lip. 'And if I were to say that you wouldn't be...er...taking advantage...?'

'My answer would still be the same.' As she flinched, his hand pressed her flat, forcing her to meet the charged glitter of his eyes. 'Do you think that I no longer want you? That is not the case. But once you said that I demeaned you, and I did. How could I not? Our marriage goes nowhere. It can go nowhere,' he spelt out harshly. 'We have no future together.'

'You never saw one!' Polly was torn by an agony that was almost physical.

His fingers slid slowly from her shoulder. 'No, I did not. You love children, and I—I have been through that war once with a woman, and I know too well its end. Even with love it could not work.'

In the chaos of those early days at Ladybright, it hadn't occurred to her that Raschid was seeing her with children for the first time. But even registering that rare betrayal of his vulnerability, she was beaten back into a passion of pain by his concluding statement. He was talking about Berah—Berah, who exerted the same deep hold on him in death as she had alive, and that was the real reason in her opinion why he had no room for Polly in his life.

'I don't want to hear about her. She was weak and selfish, and she wasn't a saint.' As anger and hurt clawed cruelly at her, the last remnants of her control came crashing down. 'And she's ruined you for anybody else!'

Perceptibly he curbed the anger hardening his facial muscles. 'I know you mean no disrespect. Had you any real understanding of how desperately unhappy she was, you wouldn't speak like that. She did not ruin me. If anything, it was I who destroyed her. I watched her change from a contented and uncomplicated girl into a bitterly insecure and disturbed woman.'

'But I ... am ... not ... her!' Her throat was thick and full. 'And I love you.'

A profound silence enclosed the involuntary spill of her words. She shut her eyes tightly, physically willing the clock to turn back and reclaim her confession.

'You are distraught. You do not know what you are saying.' Raschid's withdrawal was instantaneous, a cold wind across tender flesh.

She was too bitterly upset to heed the warning. 'Don't I? It may be an emotion foreign to you in relation to me, but I know how I feel!'

Dark blood had burnished his high cheekbones. Slashing a hand down in finality, he reached for his woollen *tobe*. 'No more. In the morning you will regret this.'

'All I regret,' she framed with a shaky sincerity that had its own dignity, 'is falling in love with a man who is afraid to feel anything for any woman. What did she do to you?' she continued painfully.

A tremor racked him. He lifted his clear, compelling eyes from the ground and challenged hers fiercely. She

knew that he hated her for witnessing his naked emotion
and probing clumsily at wounds that had never healed.
After four years he couldn't even bear to talk about
Berah. In inflicting pain on him, Polly suffered doubly,
for she felt his pain as if it was her own. In stark fear,
she had lost her head, for if he shut her out of his bed,
he shut her out altogether. Her heart belonged to him,
but it was an unsolicited gift he had cast aside without
hesitation. Then who wanted to find love where they felt
none? Her love had no intrinsic value. What had she
believed she might awaken with her foolish admission?
Pity would have heaped coals of fire on her.

What did she do to you? He hadn't answered. Polly
could have answered for him. She had died.

Some timeless period on in that endless, hellish night,
Raschid returned. In silence she lay there until dawn
spread a grey pall of light. She must have slept then, for
the racket of rotor blades rudely awakened her and the
heat that had damply slicked her limbs told her the day
must now be well advanced. As she sat up, she was disconcerted to find Raschid seated at the corner of the
bed, his probing scrutiny mercilessly pinned to her.

'The plane . . .?' she queried.

'Aldeza is a half-day's ride from here. By air it will
take less than half an hour.'

She fiddled with the fringed edge of the rug. 'You're
still speaking to me.' It was a limp attempt at humour.

'Strange as it may seem in the light of recent events,
we are not, I hope, undisciplined children.' The cool
controlled politeness with the edge of satire she dreaded
was back. A tortured sense of frustration consumed her.
The barriers were erected again with a vengeance.

At first glimpse Aldeza stole Polly's breath away. At the
second it stole her heart. An exotically beautiful white
marble palace of crowned domes and slender minarets,
it shimmered a dozen tranquil reflections in the stilled

waters of the silent stone fountains dotting its superb frontage. On every side lush gardens of shaded arbours and trellised walks beckoned and vibrant roses of every imaginable hue flourished against the oasis of greenery. The Palace of the Fountains was a polished jewel enhanced by an exquisite setting.

Built four hundred years ago by an ancestor of Raschid's, the hilltop palace had lain empty for over fifty years. Polly couldn't understand why nobody in the family had previously mentioned its existence to her. Surely they must visit this beautiful place? Before they entered the building, she darted over to a glorious climbing rose and snapped off a single, unfurling bud.

'Why don't the fountains work?' she asked.

'I believe they must have fallen into disrepair. That can be rectified,' Raschid assured her.

'Oh, don't make that effort on my account!' she snapped.

Doors stood wide on a huge, deserted entrance hall, lined by carved pillars. An army could have marched before them. Mosaic tiles in every shade from lapis lazuli to deepest emerald patterned every surface with spectacular effect. 'This is out of this world,' Polly said reverently, cricking her neck and turning slowly. 'I've never seen anything...'

'Quite so reminiscent of an Arabian Nights fantasy?' As he watched her, an irreverent grin banished his austerity. 'At last I have pleased!'

Resenting his ability to tease her when she was employing conscious effort to conceal her absolute misery, she moved away. 'Why is it empty?'

'The situation is remote and not easily accessible. In the days before hunting was prohibited, my father would bring parties of guests here. But now Aldeza has become a white elephant. When the family desire a change of scene they head for the Costa del Sol and the nightlife.

We have a villa there.' He paused. 'Did I tell you that Asif and Chassa are in Spain at present?'

'No.'

'I believe that their problems are at an end,' he remarked.

Polly folded her arms. 'Good for them. Who last lived here?'

She could feel his frown on her back. But his family were not her family, and he had slapped her down on the one occasion she had dared to believe otherwise. She would not be drawn now to invite another snub.

'My grandmother, Louise. She lived here alone for many years.'

She spun. 'Louise? That's not an Arabic name.'

Raschid looked at her in surprise. 'She was French. I thought you would have known that.'

'It never fails to amaze me what you imagine I might magically know without being told,' she said tartly.

'Or me of what you might learn did you but ask.'

Her teeth gritted. 'I am asking. How did you acquire a French grandmother?'

'Her father was an anthropologist, who came here to write a book on the nomadic culture. Louise worked as his assistant. My grandfather, Salim, only met her once to fall violently in love with her.' His firm mouth curled dismissively. 'Much happiness it brought to either of them!'

'It sounds romantic to me,' observed Polly.

'They broke up within two years and spent the next fifteen living apart. Does that sound romantic?' Raschid threw her a sardonic smile. 'But of course I would not know what might fall within that category, would I?'

'You said it, and if he was one bit like you, I'm not...' The curious sound of a stick tapping across the tiled floor whipped her head around.

# CHAPTER NINE

A WIZENED little old lady, shrunken by age into a bent bundle of black cloth, was approaching them, flapping a hand to harry the servants hurrying behind her. As she creaked down low before Raschid, he tried unsuccessfully to persuade her from the attempt, but down she went, jabbering in shrill excitement, her blackbird-bright eyes avidly pinned to them both.

Under the voluble onslaught of her emotional greeting, Raschid grew oddly tense. His brow furrowed, a curious expression set his hawkish profile for a split second before he produced a distinctly strained smile. Fingers of colour had overlaid his complexion when he turned to Polly. 'This is Ismeni. She is very old, and her mind wanders now. Would you give her that rose you carry?' He answered her bewilderment with a charged glance. 'She believes it is for her because she imagines you to be Louise. The poor creature is quite convinced that we are my grandparents,' he related under his breath.

'She's *what*?'

'Dispute will only distress her, but indeed it is a melancholic misapprehension on which to begin our stay,' he told her.

Tickled pink by his discomfiture, Polly suddenly smiled and bent to bestow the rose on the weeping Ismeni. A clawlike hand clutched hers and dry lips pressed to her knuckles. Raschid gently raised the old lady. Snapping his fingers, he summoned two of the servants, stonily studying the floor nearby, to attend to her. To Polly's amusement, Ismeni drove them back with a staccato stream of commands and bustled round again to usher her and Raschid personally into a lofty-ceilinged salon, adorned by some very fine pieces of period furniture.

'Why did she want the rose?' whispered Polly. 'There are thousands of them outside.'

'Louise planted them. Roses have special significance for Ismeni. Her former mistress allowed no one to pick them.'

'Lord, I feel like a vandal now!'

A disorientating smile slashed his lips. 'Not at all. The gift of a rose from my grandmother must have been a signal honour. Why am I whispering? You are contagious, Polly.' Then he raised a brow. 'Or is this the result of being welcomed as the resurrected? Ismeni must see a doctor, though I doubt if much may be done.'

'At least she seems happy.' Polly sat down on a delicate gilded sofa with all the comfort of a rock-face. 'Tell me the rest of the story,' she pressed. 'I assume that Louise had blue eyes.'

'Yes. She was fair, though not as fair as you.' His gaze strayed to the glistening veil of silver hair tumbling round her shoulders, lingered ruefully on her attentive stillness. 'It isn't a happy story. Salim was young and hot-headed. He persuaded Louise to marry him after only a handful of meetings, but religious and cultural differences soon divided them. After my father was born, Louise came here to live. She came on a visit and she refused to return.'

Polly frowned. 'What did he do to make her do that?'

'What did they have in common, Polly?' Raschid shrugged noncommittally. 'She hated the way of life here. She was educated, well travelled and independent. She had enjoyed a freedom which was denied to her in marriage. She couldn't adjust to the cloistered existence of the harem. She was also a devout Catholic, and the continued practice of her faith did not recommend her to female relatives who already resented Salim's choice of a foreign bride.'

'I wonder how much of an effort he made to help her adjust.'

'Who knows? My grandfather was greatly angered when she refused to return to him. He took a second wife,' Raschid divulged grudgingly.

'My goodness!' gasped Polly.

'Mirsa, my uncle Achmed's mother,' Raschid supplied. 'Undoubtedly there was a desire for revenge in the speed with which he made that marriage, but he was quite within his rights according to his faith. If he wanted to punish Louise he must have suffered for the impulse, for she never forgave him for it.'

'How could she have?' Polly demanded hotly.

Raschid sighed. 'When my father was six, Mirsa died in a cholera epidemic. In the intervening years my grandparents had scarcely spoken. When he came here, she remained in the harem and he would see his son and not her. But after a suitable period of mourning, he approached Louise and begged her to return to him as his wife. She refused him. There was no forgiveness in her heart.'

'How could there have been? He spends six years with another woman, fathers a child and then condescends to ask her back?' she interrupted.

Exasperation clouded Raschid's gaze. 'He could not abandon Mirsa after marrying her. He still loved Louise. It must have cost him much pride to make that approach when she had deserted him in the first instance. It was my father's belief that my grandmother still cared for him. However, they did not enjoy a reconciliation. When he was here, she kept to her own apartments. She died of a lung infection, and it is a fact that he grieved very deeply on her death and he did not remarry,' he completed drily.

Moisture was clogging Polly's vision. She grimaced over her silliness, but it really was the most miserable story. 'It was all his fault.'

'I knew it would make you sad, but why it should also make you argumentative, I do not know. Must we engage in partisan sympathies with two people who died even before we were born?' He studied her ruefully. 'Doesn't that strike you as a trifle fanciful?'

Embarrassed by her sentimentality, she got up and wandered restively across the room. But she was thinking of Louise, making a stand at Aldeza in what must have been a cry for help and rewarded for her defiance by her husband's cruel resort to another woman.

'For goodness' sake, Polly, they couldn't live together. They were unsuited,' Raschid pronounced with finality.

An edged laugh fell from her, and she whipped round, her luminous eyes embittered. 'Like us? Isn't that how you would describe us? Once he'd tired of her, he didn't give a damn about her feelings, and I bet that every inch of the way he laid down the law on exactly what suited him. And altered his arguments accordingly! Are you telling me that you can't see parallels, Raschid?'

He sent her a driven glance from shimmering blue eyes. 'In the mood that you are in, I will not argue with you.' Icy constraint marked him. 'You are not yourself.'

But she was what his handiwork had made of her. He had forced a need into her very skin that did not neatly vanish at his command. He had roused emotions that even she could not control. And now she was to switch off and meekly accept the status quo, swallowing the face-saving lies he had considerately put within her reach.

He didn't want to take advantage of her; that falsehood had been proven. They had no future because he couldn't give her a child. That was her decision, not his. That he had not even given her that option proved his insincerity. Their marriage had been just a game for Raschid, a cruel sexual game for a highly sexed male.

He had used her—he had admitted it. Now he didn't want the messy complications. Damn you! she thought, you're tearing me apart! He was standing there mentally willing her to match his composure and his control called up the devil inside her. Polly was swept by an incensed and bitter urge to smash it.

'You won't argue with me?' With one hand she lifted a vase and slung it across the room, where it shattered noisily against the wall two feet to the left of him. He hadn't moved an inch. Dazed by her wanton destructiveness and the violence which had suddenly forced a passage through her, she licked her lips. 'Now we've got something relevant to argue about...'

Anger and disbelief vibrated from him. Her breath loosed in a sobbing sound. 'I'm sorry,' she muttered.

'Come here,' ordered Raschid.

'No!'

Her judicious refusal seemed to land a second after he reached her. If she had wanted a reaction, she was getting it now. He had her cornered. Stepping sideways, she met with steel-clad fingers braced against the cold wall. 'In all my life,' he gritted, 'no man and no woman has ever raised a hand to me!'

'I wasn't aiming at you!' she protested.

His hands clamped round her wrists. He wasn't listening. 'With the exception of you.'

In one inexorable motion he dragged her against him. His aggressively masculine proximity inflamed her already stirred emotions. Whatever he might have intended to say was forgotten when he stared down at the breathlessly parted invitation of her lips, the unwitting softness of her eyes. Later she didn't know how it happened. One minute he was glowering down at her, the next his mouth was plundering hers with an explosive hunger that demolished her shaky defences.

Rage and wild ecstasy were one in that embrace. Passionately she yielded to him, melting into boneless acquiescence against his hard male contours. He kissed her until a thunderbeat of crazy excitement had her trembling in his hold, and then he jerked back, thrusting her away from him. Bright sunlight hid his virile figure from her bemused stare. At the far end of the room a servant entered with a tray of refreshments.

'Forgive me,' Raschid ground out in a stifled undertone.

Polly could not forgive him. She hadn't seen the servant, dismissed by a mere motion of his hand; all she had tasted was the raw vehemence of Raschid's repudiation. The drag in the atmosphere was intense. She was drained like a defeated bird who has beaten its wings too long against the bars of a cage. Last night in a fit of emotional insanity she had confessed her deepest and most private feelings, and had set the stage for her own humiliation. To rise above that awareness now in receipt of another rejection was impossible for her. It was over, it had long been over; he had tried to tell her that diplomatically last night. How many times did he have to hurt her before she would accept the truth? You couldn't make someone love you, you couldn't make them care.

'I don't think you really understand how I feel. Perhaps I did not express myself well last night, but you must believe that for a long time I have considered only what was best for you,' he breathed starkly.

Disgusted at this piece of hypocrisy, Polly refused even to look at him. 'Will you get someone to show me to my room?' she said coldly.

He uttered her name as though it was torn from him. Only when the dead silence had ticked painfully on did he fulfil her request. He didn't argue her retreat—he had to be relieved by it. Tact and exquisite manners were not enough to drain the discomfort from dealing with a wife who did not want to let go and who had the most embarrassing habit of opening her mouth to say exactly what she thought.

Half an hour later she lay in the barbaric splendour of a sunken tiled bath, an escape from the excessive attention of several twittering female servants. This was an old-style harem, accessible by a single corridor and sealed behind grilled windows, *mesharabiyah* screens and an iron-barred gate. An unearthly silence had reigned through the intersecting and richly ornate rooms. They had crossed an echoing expanse, an eerie green marble grotto of still water and shadowy archways. Thinking of Louise sentenced to solitary exclusion here from the outside world made Polly shudder. At least she would be going home eventually, she thought in miserable self-consolation.

She dismissed the servants hovering in the bedroom. The bed was enthroned on three shallow marble steps and on it rested an ensemble that would not have shamed a Twenties film starlet. Surveying the shimmering silk nightdress and the ridiculously extravagant azure satin wrap with its silly feathered trimmings, Polly squirmed. It had been dug from the bottom of her case and pressed. Just three weeks ago that over-the-top glamour had caught her wistful eye in the window of an exclusive lingerie boutique near her father's hospital, and in a weak moment she had splashed out. For Raschid. Cruel reality had shredded her embarrassing daydreams but, since she didn't know where the rest of her clothes were, she had to put the outfit on.

A meal was brought to her while she rested on a tasselled ottoman. By then she had examined her surroundings. She was in Louise's rooms, falsely occupying apartments that Ismeni appeared to have conserved to the best of her ability. Faded sepia photographs adorned the elegant writing desk. A tiny bud vase there contained the rose she had given the old lady. An opened drawer had revealed yellowing notepaper, envelopes inscribed with spiky handwriting and tied with ribbon. On the dressing table monogrammed silver brushes awaited a ghostly hand. It was decidedly creepy.

Shortly after nine Ismeni appeared bearing a tiny cup of hot chocolate. With gnarled hands she turned down the bed and lovingly smoothed pillows embroidered with tiny roses. She became agitated when Polly tried to communicate with her. Polly had to steel herself to get into Louise's bed. A shiny crescent moon speared pearly, indeterminate shadows into the room and the quiet folded in. Twenty minutes later Polly rebelliously threw the covers back and got up. Dammit, she didn't have to play up to Ismeni's batty delusions to this extent! The old dear wouldn't know if she sneaked off to find another bed, because frankly the hair was starting to prickle at the back of her neck. The unhappy Louise's spectral presence had got a death-grip on Polly's imagination.

Leaving the room, she almost tripped over the bundle sleeping across her doorway wrapped in a rug. Shoe-button eyes came alive, and Ismeni gave her a toothless grin. Startled into a gasp, Polly was guiltily put in mind of one of Macbeth's witches. Tottering upright, the old lady seemed unsurprised to see her. Bowing low as if a command had been issued, she started down the dark corridor in the most peculiar stealthy fashion without putting on a single light.

After a moment's hesitation Polly followed. Traversing the grotto room, Ismeni disappeared into the shadows where she opened a door, motioning Polly to precede her. Glimpsing a narrow, curving staircase, her curiosity fairly caught by now, Polly went ahead—then flinched when the heavy door thudded shut behind her, sealing her into Stygian gloom. In vain she struggled to open it from the inside. Incredibly, there was no handle.

'Ismeni!' she yelled frantically.

There was no answer. Unable to see an inch ahead in the musty darkness, she had to feel her passage clumsily up the climbing wall. There were thirty-two precariously narrow steps. At the top her palms met solid wood. In claustrophobic panic she pushed with all her might, and the panel swung out with a noisy creak. Her own momentum catapulted her forward into the dark room, and she stubbed her bare toes painfully on something and went down with a crash and a very unladylike epithet to clutch her throbbing foot in inexpressible agony.

Sudden light illuminated the scene. Aghast, she stared at Raschid, who had leapt out of a chair by the window. If Polly was astonished to see him, he was equally astonished to see her. His hand dropped back from the tall Persian lamp. He stood there poised, his shirt hanging unbuttoned and loose from the jeans sleekly outlining his long, straight legs, his brown feet bare.

Recognising Ismeni's gruesome mistake with scarlet-cheeked chagrin, Polly mumbled, 'I must have taken a wrong turning somewhere.'

Raschid was strangely unresponsive. His brilliant blue eyes fanned over the opulence of her attire. His lashes fanned down. He seemed to breathe in very, very slowly before he unfroze and strode over to crouch down beside her. 'My apologies. You...er...startled me. Your foot...nothing is broken?'

Above her averted head an anguished twitch threatened his steel-set mouth.

'I'm sorry if I disturbed you,' muttered Polly.

Absently he plucked a cobweb from her feathers. 'I was not in bed. I went for a ride and...came back.' His voice fractured and slurred as she released her grip on her foot and the over-large wrap lurched off one pale shoulder to reveal the utter transparency of the whisper-thin garment underneath. 'You came to me...and it went wrong,' he murmured with husky suddenness. 'I know how this feels. You must not be embarrassed. It was very sweet, and I am very touched.'

On the brink of glacially disabusing him of the notion that, not content to trail him home to Dharein, she had decided to lay siege to him in his bedroom as well, Polly looked up, connecting with the electrifying intensity of his eyes. Her heartbeat accelerated as if he had turned an ignition key. His forefinger unsteadily skimmed an untidy strand of silver back behind her ear.

'And also it is very exciting,' he muttered thickly.

Her brain was in limbo. That straying hand was gliding a tantalising path down over the column of her extended throat and she wanted to move into the warmth of that hand. The potent male scent of him intoxicated her. 'Ex...citing?' she echoed.

'An invitation from one so shy.' Lean fingers banded round her slender forearms to tug her relentlessly closer. 'Your generosity shames me. My pride would have kept me from you, but now that you are here...'

'Yes?' she croaked.

'I cannot refuse you when night after night I have ached for you.' His voice was uneven, sibilant. 'And to what avail? I cannot deny you. *Insh'allah.*'

The tip of his tongue traced the sensitive curve of her lower lip, and she shivered violently. *Insh'allah.* If the Lord wills it, so it will be. *Insh'allah.* This happens because it is already written. Raschid captured her hands, guiding them down over warm, bronzed flesh, roughened by a crisp haze of dark hair. Beneath her tentative caress he shuddered, venting a shaken groan of satisfaction. He threw back his head, his darkened eyes fiercely searching. 'Is this what you really want?'

A torture chamber would not have extracted the admission that she had not arrived under her own steam. 'You've...er...changed your mind?'

Her nervous question elicited a rueful laugh. He pulled her to him, sealing her soft curves hungrily to his male heat. 'Polly, I have never been in doubt of what I want. I have only doubted what was fairest to you, and never more than when I saw you in another man's arms—a man whom you have always been ready to love, a man whom you might have married had I not come into your life. It did not seem unlikely to me that you should turn to him when I had neglected you, and I wanted to hate you for it,' he breathed roughly into her hair, 'because I did not feel I had the right to tear you from him. But now I find there is little of the martyr in me.'

Slumbrously he studied her as he got up, lithely carrying her with him. Silk sheeting cooled her back, as he laid her down as if she was fashioned of spun glass. All that she grasped from that hail of sudden words was that his jealousy of Chris had been much more deep-rooted than she had ever suspected.

'You are sure?' he repeated.

As she nodded, still a little dazed by what was happening, his tautness evaporated. He smiled, and her pulses went haywire. He bent over her and the thrumming in the air sizzled with pure electricity. 'When you are near or far,' he confessed, 'I burn for you, night and day. No woman has ever had that power over me.'

Sadness entered her briefly. Berah reigned on upon her pedestal, divorced from earthly pleasures. The incandescent chemistry of the bedroom was Polly's only weapon. A few weeks ago she would have scorned it. An inner voice jeered at her present frailty. Was this how she would hold him? With the desire that could make him swerve from cool logic in a moment's temptation? Quote fatalism in smooth excuse for his inconsistency? She wouldn't listen to that voice. He didn't love her, and that wasn't fair, but there were many unfair things in life. This would be enough, she told herself squarely. This time—it would be enough.

His mouth dipped to caress the tempting pink-budded breast invitingly shaped by silk. Her fingers speared deep into his black hair, holding him to her, for she was racked by an intolerable hunger. Almost roughly he found her mouth again, his hands hard on her hips as he raised her to the thrusting evidence of his arousal beneath the tight denim. Passion flared white-hot and uncontrollable and sealed them together. What followed was the most indescribable physical pleasure Polly had ever experienced.

A rapped-out Arabic command awakened her. Peeping sleepily over Raschid's restraining arm, she was just in time to see Ismeni vanish through the same concealed panel she had entered by the night before.

'That woman, she is crazy!' Raschid declared with a distinct lack of charity. 'She actually crept in here to try and waken you up and trail you out of my bed—then she argues with me. Why should I care about my wife being found in my bed? Where else should she be? Why should I hide this?'

Polly blushed fierily. 'I hope you didn't upset her.'

'Upset her? When I told her that you were staying, she smiled smugly at me. So why did she argue?'

Polly was having some very strange ideas about what Raschid's grandparents had got up to in the dead of night when everybody else thought they weren't speaking. It was time for confession. Polly remained mute. Raschid had succumbed to that wildly seductive siren who had shamelessly thrown herself at his head last night. Now was not the time to stand up and be counted as a fraud. Exciting, she savoured blissfully. She would give Ismeni the most enormous bunch of roses. 'She still thinks I'm Louise,' she said.

'Are you seriously suggesting that my grandfather kicked his wife out of bed at dawn like a concubine...'

'How do you know he didn't?'

'By what I know of my grandmother he would not have survived to see the sun come up,' he whipped back drily. 'In any case, they never lived here together.'

'But he visited.'

'They were separated,' he reminded her.

As silence fell, uncertainty reclaimed her. The old lady's early-morning visit had taken the spotlight off their renewed intimacy. Suddenly she was afraid that Raschid might regret the night that had passed.

Veiled eyes tabulated her fluctuating expression. 'There's something I must say...' he began.

'Don't!' she rushed in nervously.

'You cannot inhabit an ivory tower forever.' As his mouth quirked, his thumb gently mocked the protective down-sweep of her lashes. 'I won't talk of our parting again, but that option must always remain open to you.'

In astonishment her eyes flew wide, drowned in the proximity of dense blue. 'You think I need that option?'

A powerful wave of emotion stirred her. In a few words Raschid removed her deepest fear. He settled back against the tumbled pillows and shifted a sinuous shoulder, sudden constraint marking his firm mouth. 'Who can foretell the future? We must be realistic,' he murmured. 'You are very young now, but some day you will want a child. That desire will take you as surely as the dawn follows darkness, and human nature being what it is, what you know you cannot have you will want all the more. But in denying what is between us, I was trying to avoid that dilemma, I was making the decision for you.'

'That wasn't your right,' Polly muttered shakily.

'I don't want you to be foolishly blind, *aziz*.'

She didn't know how to answer him. What he said was true. It would be some time in the future when she really came to terms with the impossibility of ever bringing her own baby into the world. As she sat up a twinge of nausea irritated her and automatically she lay back again, lost in her serious thoughts. Whatever regrets or pangs might seize her some day, she would keep them to herself. Thanks to Berah she would have to keep them to herself completely. Berah's failure to accept the situation had left Raschid vulnerable, and Raschid, to put it mildly, did not cope very well with the ignominy of vulnerability. He was much more likely to walk away from any relationship which might expose that weak spot. Was that savage pride of his all that had kept him from her? Oh, how much she wanted to believe that, but in her heart she could not believe it. He had had the power to deny her because she did not have the power to inspire the uncritical love and loyalty he had awarded Berah. Why was she upsetting herself like this? She had enough love for both of them, and, aware of his tension, she muttered something trite about crossing that bridge when or if they came to it.

'You know, there's something that I've always been curious about,' she admitted, eager to leave that other subject behind. 'What did you and your father argue about on our wedding day?'

A sudden, unexpected smile banished his serious aspect. 'Is that important now?'

Her bosom swelled with chagrin. 'It was about me, then,' she condemned. 'You were complaining about having to marry me, weren't you?'

He burst out laughing. 'Polly, your imagination is an unfailing source of entertainment! Very well,' he capitulated with veiled eyes, 'I shall tell you what I was told that day. There was never an assassination attempt on my father's life, and the promise made was not made with serious intent.'

'There was never an assassination attempt? But that's impossible!' Polly exclaimed.

'Your father mistook one of the guards for an assassin.' The faintest tremor roughened Raschid's explanation. 'When he dragged my father to the ground, the guard concerned shot at him, believing that he was assaulting mine.'

'But it can't have happened like that,' she argued shakily.

'I am afraid it did. My father was naturally relieved that Ernest sustained only a minor injury. Fearing that a serious diplomatic incident might result from the misunderstanding, my father allowed Ernest to believe that he had saved his life, and he made that pledge in part jest.'

Setting the incongruous truth beside her memory of her father's overweening delight in recounting the story of his one hour of heroic valour, Polly was almost overtaken by an irreverent tide of mirth. 'Dad must never find out the truth,' she whispered tautly.

'When your father requested an interview with mine, he assumed that he was coming to request that the promise be fulfilled, and it was then that he had enquiries made into your background,' Raschid went on. 'Having an undutiful son determined to remain a widower, and being impressed with what he learnt of you, he turned the situation to his advantage.'

'It was very cruel of him to tell you the truth...' Suddenly she went off into gales of laughter, unable to hold it any longer. 'Oh, I wish I'd been there!' she gasped. 'I'd love to have seen your father's face when mine hurled him down on the ground... he must have been absolutely raging!'

'I confess that at the time I was not very amused.' Laughing now himself, Raschid caught her to him, rakish eyes brightly appraising her. 'But now I would concede that he chose you very well.'

He possessed her parted lips in a blindingly hungry kiss, glancing down at her to murmur mockingly, 'By Allah, I have missed you, but you will not have the advantage of distance again. When next I go abroad, you will come with me. You have become indispensable to my comfort, *aziz*.'

Polly touched the heights of happiness in the following week. Every morning they went out riding, and under Raschid's patient tutelage she lost the nervous unease on horseback which had been instilled in her by her father's neck-or-nothing expectations when she was a child. The third morning they returned to the soft rush of water. The fountains were playing again. Raschid had had the ancient plumbing overhauled to please her.

She was enjoying a kaleidoscopic desert sunset from the vantage point of the terraced gardens one evening when he came to find her. The grey gravel plain surrounding the palace's hilly basalt setting was bathed in illusory gold and scarlet. The bleak, enduring mystery of the wilderness possessed a savage beauty and an endless, fascinating variation of colour, shape and texture that reminded her potently of Raschid.

'You look very pensive,' he commented.

He had had work to do this afternoon. The plane had come in, bringing the mail, and then for some reason it had come back again later. When Polly had walked outside, Raschid had accompanied her on a walk through the gardens. She suspected that he was afraid she had felt neglected, left to her own designs for a few hours. Now here he was again.

Gracefully she arose from the stone seat. 'I was just relaxing,' she said.

'Or were you thinking that it is Christmas Eve and you are far from home? No snow, no holly, no roaring log fires, no stocking,' he teased, rather unfeelingly, she felt, for she was hopelessly sentimental about Christmas.

'I'm a little old for a stocking,' she muttered repressively.

'I suppose you are.' Raschid flashed her a slow smile. 'I almost forgot—we have visitors.'

'Visitors?' Polly exclaimed in dismay.

He gripped her hand when she would have parted from him in the hall. 'You will do very nicely as you are.'

As he guided her determinedly into the salon, she faltered in her steps several feet into the room. Her dazed scrutiny climbed the height of an eight-foot pine tree shimmering with starry lights and glittering baubles. The carpet beneath was heaped with gaily wrapped parcels. Somewhere in the background the strains of 'Deck the Halls,' erupted loudly.

Strong arms encircled her from behind. 'Have I only made you homesick? I would have invited your family, but your father is not fit enough to travel yet.'

Her eyes filled and she swallowed thickly. 'You did this for me?'

Raschid turned her round. 'It is a small thing if it makes you happy.'

The pleasure of having overwhelmed her showed in his eyes alone. His head descended in slow motion and she stretched up instinctively for his lips to encircle hers, something vague about visitors receding into her subconscious as wildfire raced through her veins. He lifted his head, still holding her close. 'I love you,' he whispered half under his breath.

She didn't look up. She didn't believe him. She wished he had kept quiet, although it was herself that she ought to blame. By thoughtlessly hurling her love at him, she had made him uncomfortable, she had made him feel that he had to respond. And with such conviction he did it too, she reflected, torn between pain and amusement. He dropped it in a constrained, unsophisticated aside. He didn't lie very well.

Somebody coughed noisily. Raschid jerked back from her.

'Would you like us to go out and come in again?' Asif grinned from the doorway with Chassa by his side. 'Then again, I'm not that easily shocked.'

Chassa smiled at Polly's astonishment. 'I hope that you don't mind that we've invited ourselves to Christmas lunch?'

'How could she? We brought it with us, along with a Swiss chef. Airsick, by the way. Just as well he has got until tomorrow to get his act together,' Asif laughed.

'Chassa dressed the tree. Have you any idea how much trouble it was to transport that tree out here?'

Warmly embracing Polly, Chassa whispered, 'Don't listen to him. Raschid arranged it all, and we have had a lot of fun helping him to surprise you.'

It was a wonderful evening. Delighted by the efforts Raschid had made on her behalf, Polly felt her pleasure was increased by the awareness that she really was accepted as a part of his family. Chassa bubbled with an effervescence which Polly would never have associated with her a brief five weeks ago. She was a different woman, while Asif, once he had finished showing off, seemed curiously quieter. But whatever had strained their marriage had clearly been dealt with and set behind them. Chassa glowed with the confidence of a woman who knew she was loved.

When the other couple left them alone at midnight Polly could no longer resist the heaps of presents. Raschid had even arranged for her family's gifts to be collected in London and flown out. By one o'clock she was in a welter of torn wrapping paper under his indulgent eye, dazed by the extravagance of all that he had bought her and hard put to it to understand how he had contrived to do so with only a telephone at his disposal.

'All I've got for you is an anthology of poetry, and it's not even wrapped,' she confided shakily. 'I wasn't sure if I was even going to give it to you. I thought you might think I was being silly.'

Laughing, he gathered her up in his arms. 'You are my Christmas present, but if you are about to start crying again I shall leave you under the tree!'

'I'm so happy,' she sniffed, and it hit her then, a piercing, frightening arrow of foreboding as if she was offending some jealous fate by daring to be so happy. 'I don't think I ever want to leave here.'

The stark fear in her eyes had covertly engaged his attention, to etch a faint frown line between his brows. 'What is really wrong, Polly?' he asked.

'Wrong?' she gulped, staving off that horrible feeling that had briefly attacked her and knowing that she was being ridiculous to pay heed to it. Tensely she laughed. 'I was just trying to work out where I'll ever wear all that jewellery!'

'There is a State banquet next month and there is Paris next week,' Raschid murmured into her hair. 'But that was not really what was worrying you, was it?'

Cursing his perception, she buried her face in his shoulder. 'I can't help wondering how Dad will bear up to a festive season without parties,' she lied. 'I hope he'll be sensible.'

'I'm sure he will be. We'll find time to visit again soon,' he promised, his tone ever so slightly cool. But Polly didn't notice. She was thinking what a silly fool she would be to let insecurity plague her, and she looked up at him with a bright smile.

# CHAPTER TEN

IT WAS the day after Boxing Day when Polly bounced exuberantly out of bed to go riding and instead keeled over in a dead faint at Raschid's feet. Bedlam had broken out when she resurfaced. Zenobia, who had been flown out with the clothes Polly had required several days earlier, was down on her knees weeping. Raschid was biting out harsh comments to some unfortunate out of view and from the corridor outside came the babble of excitable voices, signifying the gathering of the servants scenting a drama.

'Lie still.' Before she could sit up to sheepishly announce her recovery, Raschid was pressing a restraining hand to her shoulder. 'You are not to move until the doctor arrives.'

'Where are you going to get a doctor from?'

He sighed. 'I had already arranged for Mr Soames to see Ismeni this morning. Now he will see you as well.'

'But we're supposed to be leaving today,' Polly argued. 'And I don't need a doctor.'

'Have you no respect for your health?' he demanded. 'Be grateful that I have!'

Expelling his breath, he sat down beside her. 'You scared the heart from my body. Repetition had not accustomed me to this habit of yours,' he said, attempting a taut smile. 'But don't worry. I am sure it is nothing serious.'

His restless pacing over the next few hours told her his imagination was roaming at large over a list of killer diseases. But it didn't occur to Polly that she had anything to worry about. Feeling vaguely out of sorts once or twice was surely excusable with all that had been happening in recent weeks? She didn't like to say that to Raschid in case he felt that she was blaming him for it. Perhaps she had let herself get overtired, something like that.

When the doctor arrived, Raschid announced that he would stay. Polly objected and, emanating disapproval and reproach, he left them. Mr Soames was familiar and cheerful, but he threw her completely with his third question. When had she last been bedevilled by that particular female curse? It seemed shrouded in the mists of time. Raschid had been in New York ... but that had been months ago. It couldn't have been that long, it simply couldn't have been ...

Mr Soames cleared his throat. 'Haven't you suspected the cause for yourself, Your Highness? You're pregnant.' Taking her pulse, his examination complete, he missed the arrested paralysis of her face. 'I would say ten to twelve weeks, and ...'

'I can't be ... I can't be pregnant! It's just not possible!' Her interruption was a strangled squeak.

His beetling brows rose in concert. 'There's no room for doubt, Your Highness. Your condition is too well advanced.'

The intermittent nausea which had bothered her and then vanished came to mind ... her disappearing waist. She gulped, welded visually to the older man's cool professional confidence. 'Honestly? I mean ... I really am?'

The poor man probably wondered if she required a long-overdue chat about the birds and the bees. He had no idea why his announcement should reduce her to dazed incoherency. She drifted out of the rigidity of deep shock on to a euphoric plane and nodded like a vacant marionette while Mr Soames gave forth about sensible diet and regular rest and the excellence of Chassa's obstetrician. She didn't hear a word. Under the sheet her hands slunk covertly over her stomach. The hows, whys and wherefores could not preoccupy her. Somebody had made a mistake. Or whatever had been amiss had miraculously come right. Polly was in no mood to question a miracle.

A baby. She felt ten feet tall. His baby! Exultancy claimed her. She was flooded by the dizzy joy of what this news would mean to Raschid. Then a shadow briefly fell over her rapturous, sun-filled outlook. Would he mind that it was her and not Berah? No, of course he wouldn't mind. He would be simply floored by the shatteringly wonderful discovery that he was about to become a father. She couldn't wait, she just couldn't wait to tell him and see his reaction.

Having abandoned all hope of receiving an intelligible sentence from his patient, the doctor opened the door to usher in Raschid. He beamed benevolently. 'Nothing to worry about. The most natural thing in the world, and she's in excellent health. Your wife is expecting a baby.'

Overhearing the announcement, Polly was shot from her blissful anticipation. She sat up, agonisingly disappointed by the man's thoughtlessness. Raschid's back was turned to her. It must have taken him thirty seconds to speak, and she didn't catch his response, for he was showing the doctor out again. Impatiently, expectantly she awaited his return. He'd be in shock—naturally he would be.

Raschid shut the door almost clumsily behind him. He lodged by the window, his dark head slightly averted. Too overcome to look at her? Then suddenly he moved. He smashed a clenched fist with punishing force against the carved window frame. Something cracked. If her life had depended on it, Polly couldn't have produced a vocal sound.

'When were you going to tell me?' He faced her now, ashen in complexion, every harsh lineament of his bronzed features rawly defined. Silver eyes beat into hers, metallic arrows dipped in the poison of violent repulsion. 'How do you look at me still? Have you no shame?'

'Sh-shame?' she echoed.

'You think perhaps that I am so stupid that I might believe that it could be mine? Or did you think I would be so desperate to believe that I would credit that the impossible could be possible?' He could hardly get his tongue round her language, but every cruelly destructive word hit its deadly target. 'Then I grant you reason to doubt my intelligence. Though you have never told me the whole truth about him, I believed you when you said he hadn't touched you, and now...to be presented...with the proof of your...' His English failed him altogether as he struggled for mastery of himself.

Polly had turned to stone. Her backbone was ice, her eyes blank as an accident victim's. Blood dripped from his bruised hand; he could have bled all over the carpet and she could have watched in numb inaction. Something indescribably breakable had snapped inside her. Something indefinably precious had been wrenched from her. The loss of faith, hope and charity was the least of the damage.

'It's your baby.' She hated him for forcing her to make that demeaning contradiction. By the simple expedient of mentioning just how pregnant she was, she could have vindicated herself. But a freezing cold and alien anger was hollowly filling her. Would Raschid have done this to Berah? Would he have doubted her fidelity? Would he have flatly and finally pronounced that he could not be the father of her child? All the bitter resentment that Berah's unassailable position in his heart had ever aroused in her had a stranglehold on her now when her wondrous gift was repudiated with sordid and unforgivable condemnation. He was hanging himself, and a twisted, unfamiliar part of her earned an embittered satisfaction from a ringside seat on the execution.

He was breathing fast and shallowly. 'I am neither desperate nor stupid. Sterility is irreversible.' He turned away from her. He was shaking, and then he turned back. 'Comfort!' he thundered at her, his eyes razors on her pinched profile. 'Now I know what you feared—the consequences of your treachery. Is this why you came to my bed willingly here? Did you already suspect your condition? I see this all now...in its foul clarity!'

The depth of calculation he laid at her door stunned her. He didn't want to believe because he didn't want her baby any more than he had ever really wanted her. Had he cared for her at all, he would have wanted to believe no matter how hard it was to believe. Tremulously holding on to her composure, she whispered, 'I don't think that we can have anything left to say to each other. I'll be on the first flight home.'

'Home?' The savage impact of his repetition struck her like a blow from a mailed fist. 'You will never see him again, you will never go home!' He swore that like a blood oath in the hot stillness of a seething silence. 'Until I have decided how to deal with you, you will stay here.'

Polly wouldn't defend herself. Exoneration was within her reach at the mere recall of the doctor, but she wouldn't do that unless she was forced to it. The longer Raschid harboured his filthy suspicions, the harder he would fall when the truth came out, as inevitably it must. But it would be too late then for him to develop an interest in fatherhood. Nothing would change the way she felt now. This was her baby, and by hook or by crook, she would take it home to England with her. Raschid could do whatever he liked. She was finished with him. Furthermore, getting upset wasn't good for her now. She had her baby to consider. Impervious to his unbelieving stare, Polly carefully settled herself back against the pillows and rearranged the covers, ignoring his lowering, dark presence.

When he swept out, she stared into space for a long time. Then she rolled over and the hot tears coursed down her cheeks. If there was a prize for consistent stupidity, it ought to be hers. Raschid had been determined to give their marriage a front of contented respectability. He had found the magic formula by making a fuss of her for a few days. How easily she had been deceived! How amused he must have been by the speed of her surrender! The bitterness infusing her was venomous and vengeful. It was like no feeling she had ever experienced before. It was implacable. Stifling her tears, she refused to recognise the enormous pain bottled up behind her anger. Stonily she listened to the dulled whine of the plane taking off, relieved at least that Chassa and Asif had left the day before. Now she was on her own. Suddenly she sat up again as it dawned on her that Raschid had to be sharing the flight with Mr Soames, who was as likely to refer to the baby as Raschid was unlikely to show his emotions. She smiled a not very pleasant smile. There was a strong possibility that Raschid might be back before nightfall.

But nobody came. It was the next day when she learnt that Ismeni had passed peacefully away in her sleep the night before the doctor arrived. Polly learnt quite accidentally. She had been using Raschid's room, and when she went down into the harem she walked into a hive of activity. A crate was being packed with Louise's surviving possessions. Polly's shocked response to a death which surprised no one else made Zenobia anxious.

'This lady, she was very, very old and not well in the head,' the little maid murmured uncomfortably. 'The doctor said it was her heart.'

The desktop was piled high with a mound of yellowing envelopes. As a hand moved to them, Polly gasped, 'Leave them. I'll deal with those.'

Heaping them in a box, she left the servants to their work. Upset by the news of the old lady's death, Polly could not bear to stand by and watch them dismantle Ismeni's shrine to her beloved mistress. But no doubt the servants, long hampered by Ismeni's authority, were keen to springclean a majestic suite of rooms which had probably lain unused until Polly's arrival. Since the palace had enjoyed only occasional use as a hunting lodge, there couldn't have been many important female guests here over the years.

Raschid had laughed when she told him about the untouched room, and he had laughed even harder when she confessed her foolish fancies. She had had no fear of ghosts while she slept in his arms. You weren't happy here, Louise, and I am, she had thought. Had the djinns that whispered out in the lonely places of the desert overheard her vainglorious boast? Just like Louise, she was discovering the dangerous folly of loving unwisely. And just like Louise she had been left at the Palace of the Fountains in splendid isolation.

Upstairs in the salon she flicked through the letters she had saved from the wastepaper basket. Indecipherable Arabic penned by the same hand covered every envelope, and there were dozens of them. Polly replaced them neatly in the box. Someone in the family ought to examine them in case there was something of importance in them. As she set the box aside the hum of a helicopter coming in to land disturbed the quiet. Expecting Raschid and having coolly kept away from the windows, Polly was sharply disconcerted when Asif was ushered into the salon.

'Are you your brother's messenger?' she demanded glacially.

Asif looked at her momentarily as if she had lost her wits. 'Raschid does not know I am here. He wouldn't thank me for interfering like this, and I hope that we can keep this visit of mine between ourselves,' he breathed tautly.

Polly frowned. 'I can't think of a single reason why you should have come to see me.'

He took a deep breath and then dug out a cigarette. Lighting it, he inhaled slowly. 'Look—it was I who was having the affair with Francine, not Raschid,' he said abruptly. 'You know what I am talking about, you don't need to pretend. Jezra told you about her. It is the only thing that I could think of which could have caused this trouble between you and Raschid.'

Dealt the unexpected and, what was more, the most embarrassing of the unexpected, Polly felt her passage slowly down into a seat, her stunned eyes pinned to his flushed face. 'You were having an affair?'

'It is over now. You have no need to look at me like that,' Asif muttered defensively. 'When Raschid returned without you, he looked even worse than he looked when Berah died. If he has been stupidly honourable and chosen to be secretive for the sake of my marriage, then I must speak up.'

She swallowed, wondering how to tell him that he was barking up the wrong tree. 'Asif, I really...'

He straightened his shoulders. 'You must believe me, Polly. At least let me explain. She was a secretary in our Paris Embassy. I was infatuated with her. I moved her into an apartment, using Raschid's name without his knowledge,' he admitted heavily. 'When rumours reached my father's ears, Raschid was forced to cover up for me.'

'You have a fine, upstandingly moral brother!' she interposed in disgust.

Taken aback, he stared at her. 'It wasn't like that. He did it to protect Chassa. He did it to stop me doing something foolish and breaking up my marriage.' His gaze flickered from hers as his voice dropped in volume. 'And he did it because I fear our father's anger. He is very fond of Chassa, considerably less fond of me. He also expects all of us to maintain strict standards and guard against scandal. I had been in trouble before, and my father is not a forgiving man. For a long time I have been working with Raschid to persuade him that Chassa and I need not live here all the time. If he had learnt it was I who was involved with Francine, all hope of that freedom would have been gone for good.'

'I understand.' Polly's shocked anger on Chassa's behalf was softened by a brief spasm of pity for Asif. He had abandoned his dignity in his mistaken belief that this woman Francine was at the bottom of her separation from Raschid. He had no idea of what was really wrong, and she had no intention of telling him.

'And you believe me?' he pressed impatiently.

Hurriedly she nodded. 'Yes, I believe you.'

'I have trusted you with a confidence that could destroy my marriage,' he breathed. 'Chassa doesn't know about Francine and she must never know about her. I love my wife, Polly. I have come to my senses, and I will not risk losing her again. I am asking you to keep this a secret.'

Now that Polly had the entire story, she was quite convinced that Asif's request was unnecessary, for she suspected that Chassa had known all along that there was another woman in her husband's life. Chassa had also assumed that Polly would be in Raschid's confidence. Ironically, Polly was grateful that she had not been. The awareness of Asif's infidelity would not have relaxed her in Chassa's company. She forced a soothing smile. 'Naturally you can rely on my... discretion.'

'I knew you would be an understanding woman.' His fear allayed, he smiled brilliantly at her. 'With a sensibly short memory. If you have falsely accused Raschid, you had better make the first move.'

'Indeed?' she murmured expressionlessly.

His wandering attention had fallen on the box of correspondence resting on a small drum table. He lifted one of the envelopes and without hesitation extracted the notepaper within while saying, 'Be generous, else you will wait forever. You could get blood out of a stone quicker than you could get my brother to an apology, and after all, he has made a lot of firsts for you...'

'What?'

Fixedly studying the letter in his hand, he glanced up absently and then grinned. 'Furniture warehouses, flowers, meals in hotels, the swimming pool. Do you think my brother makes a habit of these things? He's about as modern as my father, but recently he's been behaving out of character. You've led him quite a dance, Polly,' he said cheerfully. 'I've never enjoyed anything quite so much as I have enjoyed watching Raschid having to pursue a woman for the first time in his life, and he's basically rather shy...'

Polly reeled. 'Sh-shy? Raschid?'

Asif was back with the evidently fascinating letter. 'Deep down. Of course, the military education and my father soon put paid to that, but he's anything but a womaniser. Never had the opportunity until that demented woman died, and after eight years of her, I expect he had gone off the notion... boy, is this hot stuff! Whoever would have thought it?' he muttered, heading on to a second letter with appetite. 'Where did they come from?'

'Your grandmother's desk.' Polly wasn't interested in the letters. 'What did you mean by demented?'

'I really shouldn't be reading these,' Asif commented. 'But I know what I'll be doing on the flight back. Wait until my father sees them! It's the dates when they were written that have the shock value.' He was tugging out more letters to examine them.

In frustration Polly said, 'Will you forget those stupid letters for a minute? What did you mean by demented?'

He stared at her. 'Do you know what these letters are? They're love letters written by my grandfather, and he was obviously getting replies. I always understood that my grandparents separated long before she died, but they must have made it up, even though she stayed here.' Finally appreciating that he did not have her full attention, he frowned. 'What do *you* mean by what do I mean by demented? Didn't you know that she ended up in one of those clinics for the mentally disturbed?'

She had turned pale. 'No, I had no idea she was really ill.'

'Raschid didn't tell you? It's not the sort of thing anybody wants to talk about, I guess,' he conceded dubiously. 'Berah was diagnosed as a manic depressive a couple of years before she died. Raschid went through hell with her.'

Polly's surprise was unhidden.

'If I'm not very charitable about her, it's because she threw herself down those bloody stairs in front of Raschid, and I know what that did to him, and I lived with what that did to Chassa,' Asif murmured roughly.

Polly looked at him strickenly. 'She committed suicide?'

'It wasn't anybody's fault, least of all Raschid's. She was supposed to be in the clinic. It was her father who took her out of it. Achmed would never accept that she was really ill, and when he realised that my father was trying to persuade Raschid to divorce her... well, obviously he didn't want that,' he said. 'He went off to Switzerland, decided off his own bat that she was normal and brought her home so that she would be there when Raschid returned from New York. What he didn't know was that Chassa was pregnant. Berah heard the servants gossiping and she'd been off her medication for twenty-four hours. Raschid was always her audience. She died in his arms.'

Polly felt sick. Ashamed of every carping thought she had ever had about Berah in her ignorance, she whispered tearfully, 'He didn't tell me.'

Asif sighed. 'Don't blame him for that, Polly. Nobody wants to remember a nightmare. He would never have divorced her. She was as obsessed by him as she was about kids. When she died, Raschid blamed himself, although he had done everything possible to help her.'

She sucked in air chokily. 'He blamed himself because he couldn't give her a child.'

Asif shifted uncomfortably. 'I don't believe a child would have made any difference. That instability must have been in Berah. It would have come out in some other way even if there had been children. I hope that Raschid accepts that now. He suffered enough with her when she was alive.'

Polly was fumbling for a handkerchief. Shorn of the smug sense of martyred piety which had buoyed her up from Raschid's departure, she wanted to put her head down and cry.

'I ought to be going.' Uneasily Asif lifted the box and she pulled herself together long enough to see him out to the plane.

How could she have believed that Raschid was not suffering too? Only now would she let herself acknowledge the agonised pain he had struggled blindly to contain in front of her. She could have turned that whole confrontation round, but she hadn't. Hatred could lie a hair's breadth from love, and she had hated him for his lack of faith. She had wanted him to suffer. She had wanted to punish him for not loving her as he had loved Berah.

He had cause to condemn her for consistently avoiding telling him the whole truth about Chris. Raschid wasn't stupid; he had suspected that there was more. She had fostered a fertile breeding ground for his suspicions to leap back to the fore. She should never have let him leave her believing those terrible things; two wrongs did not make a right.

It was early the next day when she heard the plane. Instinctively she knew that Raschid was on it. She was still in bed and she jumped up, calling for Zenobia and instructing her to say that she would be upstairs in fifteen minutes. But Raschid didn't wait. Polly was brushing her tangled hair when he appeared. He halted six feet from her, and she looked even though she didn't want to look. Senses parched of his vibrancy overwhelmed her poise, sapped her control as she set down the brush and took a seat on the ottoman behind her.

A little pale, very tense, his left hand bandaged, he was informally clad in black jeans and as physically arresting as a panther rather sheepishly at bay. Incandescent eyes travelled over her with aching slowness and she needed no words to tell her that her explanation, her proof was not required. That look was extraordinarily expressive. If only he had given it to her two days ago! she thought with helpless bitterness.

'I expect you found out while you were gathering your evidence for a court case. You would have needed a doctor's report,' Polly attacked.

Raschid had changed colour at her taunting words. He moved. 'Polly, I . . .'

'Don't you dare come near me!' she said fiercely.

Shorn of his usual sweeping aplomb, he hovered, and she bent her head, determined not to be swayed by the sight of him. She could not compete with Berah's shadow. She could not be second best. The intensity of her own feelings for him demanded more, and after all she had gone through, being accepted simply because she could give him the child he had thought he could never have, wasn't enough. 'You can skip the apologies, the heartfelt regrets and the smoothie persuasions,' she whispered painfully. 'You can have access, but I really don't think we could ever live together again.'

He shifted. 'Try to imagine how I felt.'

'Stay where you are!' Polly snapped shakily. 'I'm being sensible, and I'm never sensible when you get close.'

He drew his hand from behind his back and laid a single white rose on the carpet along with a small pink furry teddy bear. 'I am at your feet with them,' he muttered hoarsely.

Polly surveyed the offerings in horror. Her throat closed over. She had underestimated the depths to which he would sink in a tight corner. Her hand flew up to her convulsing mouth. Her eyes watered accusingly. 'I am not touched,' she spluttered. 'Do you hear me?'

He took immediate advantage of her emotional disarray by striding forward to match the declaration he had made with the action. His arms enclosed her tightly and he buried his head in her lap. 'Forgive me,' he implored gruffly. 'If I could not believe in a miracle, it is because I have never experienced one before. I would give all that I had to steal those accusations I made from your memory, but I cannot. I can only ask you to try to understand that for ten years I believed that I could not father a child. I never doubted it, and I never forgot this fact. It haunted me with Berah, and it haunted me even more after her death.'

Black silky hair, dark as a raven's wing, was brushing her clenched hands. She ached to touch him, to hold him. It was a craving that stormed through her every defence. The harsh sincerity of his plea was more than she could withstand. Her hand crept up on to his taut shoulder as she whispered, 'You hurt me so much. I was so happy, and then all of a sudden it was like a bad dream.'

Raschid looked up at her with anguished azure eyes. 'It should have been beautiful, and I spoilt it—but ten years, Polly,' he repeated, 'it is a long time. When he said you were pregnant it almost destroyed me.'

'Your first thought was that I . . .'

'My first thought was that I had driven you into his arms,' he interrupted, roughly insistent. 'I was so shocked that I could see no other explanation.'

Polly reddened. 'It wasn't all your fault,' she said ruefully. 'When I married you I did think I was in love with Chris, and when I realised that I wasn't, I just wanted to forget about it. I'd made myself so miserable for so long . . . well, it left me feeling rather stupid.'

He buried his mouth heatedly in the centre of one of her palms. 'I had seen the bond of affection between you at the wedding,' he breathed, lifting his head. 'I did not suspect you then. He was flirting with you, but you were not flirting with him. It must seem very arrogant of me, but I did not really believe that you might love him until I saw you with him at your home. Then I wanted to rip him asunder . . . slowly.'

Polly gulped. 'It was just one of those things. He didn't mean to kiss . . .'

'We have talked enough about him,' Raschid interrupted with a subdued flash in his clear gaze. 'He is unimportant. It is Berah we must talk about. It was only when I was on the plane that it occurred to me that she could have lied.'

'Lied?' she echoed.

He gave a harsh laugh. 'Yes—lied. At first it was hard for me to accept that she could have done that. Two years into our marriage she had shown very few signs of her illness. I had no reason to suspect that she could practice such an appalling deception, but I should have suspected later. I should have, but by then I had other problems with which to concern myself. I have never been honest with you about Berah. I always felt the need until now to defend her memory from criticism.'

'I can understand that. Asif explained . . .'

As Polly compressed her lips in dismay over the admission, Raschid sighed. 'It is all right—I know he was here. Having given my father those letters last night, he could not hide where he had been, and he told me exactly what he had told you. It was not all true. Asif likes to exaggerate.'

He released her hand and stood upright. 'Berah did not commit suicide. She fell, Polly. She was extremely distressed, crying, hysterical. It was an accident. I am not denying that she had suicidal impulses, but if she had wanted to die, she would not have chosen such a method. She fell,' he said again. 'But that did not make me feel that I had failed her any less. When I left you here, I flew to London.'

She frowned. 'Why?'

'To see the specialist whom she had seen,' he explained, a muscle jerking tight at the corner of his mouth. 'It was not to check up on whether or not you could be telling me the truth. I had to know. I had to know for my own peace of mind whether or not Berah had lied or somehow misunderstood, and when I spoke with that man, the irrational guilt of years left me.'

'It must have been very upsetting for you to discover that she could have done that to you,' Polly remarked brittly.

Bleakly Raschid looked back at her. 'No, it was the most wonderful thing I had ever heard in my life. It set me free of my conscience.' He moved a broad shoulder jerkily. 'You see, I never loved her. I cared for her, she was my wife, but I was never able to love her as she loved me. She would never meet me as an equal. She would not mix with other people, and she took a dislike to every member of my family. Although she was quiet with me, she was vicious with the servants. Of course she was not well, but I did not know that when we were first married. The time when I might have learned to love her went past.'

Pale with a mixture of guilt and regret, he watched her anxiously, and she knew that he had never admitted those feelings to another living soul. 'Shortly after she informed me that I was sterile,' he continued in a clipped undertone, 'it became clear that she no longer wished to share my bed. I needed her desperately then. It wasn't until I understood that she was ill that I could forgive her for that.'

So much that she had never understood was now painfully obvious to Polly. Instinctively she stood up and crossed over to him, wrapping her arms round him tightly, thinking how ironic it was that she should want to cry for Berah. Berah had lied to Raschid because she didn't want to lose him. 'She is at peace now,' she muttered against his shirt-front, drowning in the evocative heat and scent of him, the petty bite of her consuming jealousy finally laid to rest.

'But I am not at peace, *aziz*. I cannot live without you by my side,' Raschid confessed harshly. A fear and an aching loneliness that put talon claws into her heart was in his eyes as he looked down at her. 'I love you,' he said fiercely.

'Yes,' Polly mumbled shakily, seeing that so very clearly now.

'How could you have doubted it?' he groaned, enfolding her slender body to the muscular hardness of his taut length. 'I fell in love with you when you had the flu—that is not very romantic, is it? But I couldn't stay away from you, I couldn't pass the door. Just to hear the sound of your voice, to see you. I couldn't help myself. But I didn't know I was in love until I saw you with the children. Then I knew, and I fought it. How could I ask you to spend the rest of your life with me?'

She smiled tremulously. 'You can ask me.'

His dark head bent. 'I am not asking you now, I am telling you that I will never let you leave me.' Lifting her up against him, he found her mouth hungrily, and it was a long time before either of them was in the mood for conversation again.

Sleepily Polly asked about the letters Asif had carried off.

'No doubt we will hear all about them when we go back, but it seems that Louise did forgive my grandfather in the end. However, she wouldn't return to live with the rest of the family. Salim was a very proud man. He did not even want his son to realise that he had accepted her terms,' Raschid clarified, viewing her lazily with unreserved adoration. 'I think it pleased my father greatly, for he was full of it last night when I went to speak with him, but he did not get to tell me very much, for I had more important news.'

'Like what?' Polly enquired.

He grinned. 'That I am to be a father in August. I could not keep it to myself!' His smile dimmed at her sudden tension. 'It just came out, Polly. I wanted to tell everybody.'

'Well, you might have got the month right. It's more likely to be June,' she told him, but she smiled at the awareness that he had accepted the truth without the knowledge of when she had conceived.

'So soon?' he exclaimed.

Polly looked forgivably smug at his astonishment. The baby had been the eighth wonder of the world even before this; it had now added the ninth to its tally. 'And you can go and change that teddy for a blue one,' she tossed in for good measure. 'I'm convinced that I'll have a boy.'

'I don't care,' Raschid confided with a reverent hand resting on the slight curve of her stomach. 'A baby is a baby. A child—our child.'

'What did your father say?' she asked worriedly.

'Initially little. He was overjoyed into unusual silence until I explained about Berah, and then he called me all kinds of a fool for accepting her word without question. I have no doubts that the whole palace knows by now— he was shouting at the top of his voice!'

Polly relaxed until another concern gripped her. 'I suppose it won't be good news for Asif and Chassa.'

He smoothed her furrowed brow with gentle fingertips, that heart-stopping smile of his strongly in evidence. 'Asif was there, and he is jubilant. My father will no longer insist that Chassa and the children must live in Dharein. They will probably move to London or New York. It is what they have always wanted.'

Her last worry banished, she gave a euphoric little sigh. 'I suppose I ought to admit that Ismeni took me to that staircase and I didn't know where I was going.'

'I had already worked that out for myself.' Bright blue eyes skimmed her blushing face mockingly. 'And after lunch you can put on that glorious outfit again and play the scene afresh. The perfect penance, don't you think?'